"If he didn't go into the hills to prospect, then why?"

"To meet the Hawk?" Ridge suggested.

"Or to get away from him," Elena said.

He sat up, suddenly energized. Why hadn't he considered that before? Ridge should have realized his dad had been running from danger.

The next instant, a different, more alarming scenario occurred to him.

"Dad could have been drawing his killer away from the ranch. To save me, my sister and my mom. The guy he'd been arguing with did threaten the family."

"That's possible," Elena agreed. "But unfortunately, you'll probably never know."

For the first time, emotion showed in her expression. Ridge saw compassion and empathy mixed with sorrow and felt a sudden bond with her. Perhaps, like him, she'd suffered loss and had failed to receive needed closure.

Before he could respond, they heard the rumble of an approaching vehicle. Ridge pushed back from the table and stood. Elena, too. They both glanced out the kitchen window.

"The chief and Jake are here," he said, and readied himself for what would no doubt be yet another battle with law enforcement.

Cathy McDavid has been writing for Harlequin since 2005. With over sixty titles to date, she spends her days figuring out how to bring two mismatched people together, break them up and then realistically reunite them for a happily-ever-after. When not chained to the computer, she serves at the pleasure of her four-footed muses and the whims of her two adult children, all while her poor neglected husband watches from afar.

Books by Cathy McDavid

Love Inspired Suspense

Deadly Secrets

Love Inspired Mountain Rescue

Wildfire Threat
Blizzard Refuge
Mountain Storm Survival

Visit the Author Profile page at LoveInspired.com.

Deadly Secrets

CATHY McDAVID

LOVE INSPIRED SUSPENSE
INSPIRATIONAL ROMANCE

LOVE INSPIRED® SUSPENSE
INSPIRATIONAL ROMANCE

ISBN-13: 978-1-335-98018-2

Deadly Secrets

Recycling programs
for this product may
not exist in your area.

Love Inspired
22 Adelaide St. West, 41st Floor
Toronto, Ontario M5H 4E3, Canada
www.LoveInspired.com

Printed in Lithuania

MIX
Paper | Supporting
responsible forestry
FSC® C021394

Ask, and it shall be given you; seek, and
ye shall find; knock, and it shall be opened unto you.
—*Matthew 7:7*

To Pops, the best grandfather ever.
Could you have ever imagined when you rode the rails from Montreal to Arizona as a young teenager that your granddaughter would one day move to Arizona and write about the same mountains you traveled through? I miss you and love you still.

ONE

The old woman stood on her dusty concrete porch stoop and leveled an arthritic finger at Deputy Elena Tomes. Tucked in the crook of her other arm, a fat gray cat hissed and growled and dug its sharp claws into the woman's skin deep enough to draw blood. She didn't appear to notice.

"What are you going to do about it?" she demanded.

Elena silently prayed for patience. "As I explained to you when I first arrived, there's nothing I *can* do."

"That vicious dog next door keeps coming into my yard and scaring poor Peaches."

"You have to call Animal Control."

"I did. And they said because the dog wasn't on my property when they got here, all they could do was issue a verbal warning."

Elena glanced over at the neighbor's backyard where the dog in question, a white ball of corkscrew curls hardly bigger than the cat, played chase with a pair of giggling girls. Vicious? Elena doubted it. More likely the dog was defending itself against Peaches's assault.

She noted the bent chain-link fence with its many holes separating the two properties. "Maybe if you repaired the fence, the dog wouldn't get into your yard."

"Me?" the woman gasped. "Their dog is the one trespassing. Fixing the fence is their responsibility."

"Have you told them that?"

She squared her shoulders, the bony knobs visible beneath her droopy cardigan. "I have. They refuse."

"Then maybe you should take them to court. Let a judge decide. But in any case, this isn't a matter for the sheriff's department. You can't keep calling with nuisance complaints."

"Nuisance?" Vivid red splotches bloomed on her wrinkled cheeks. "I'll have you know I won't be voting for you in the next election."

Elena swallowed a sigh. "I'm not an elected official, ma'am. You're thinking of the Cochise County sheriff. I'm just a regular employee."

Elena had been hired on four months ago at the Ironwood Creek Sheriff's Substation. Her recruitment was part of the governor's new program to fill deputy vacancies with female and underrepresented candidates.

But Elena didn't explain any of that to the old woman. There was no point.

"What's the name of your supervisor?" the woman demanded. "I have half a mind to report you."

"Sergeant Deputy Jake Peterson. I can write that down for you if you want."

"Oh, trust me. I'll remember."

"If that's all, ma'am…" Elena tugged on the brim of her dark green ball cap. She didn't much like the regulation headwear, but it did protect her from the sun, relentless in this southeastern corner of Arizona even during winter.

Besides, the hat, combined with aviator sunglasses, made her look tougher and older. With her small stature and youthful features, few people took Elena seriously. That included her fellow deputies, much to her consternation.

She felt the old woman's stare burn into her as she walked to where her county-issued black-and-white SUV sat parked alongside the narrow street. Curtains parted and blinds separated as nosy people peered out their windows at the goings-on.

Elena paid them no heed and climbed into the driver's seat. There, she squeezed her eyes shut, already dreading the paperwork for this unnecessary call.

"Lord, I know You led me here for a reason, and I'm willing to wait until that reason reveals itself. But in the meantime, I could sure use a bit of encouragement."

After a moment, she sat up and radioed the station. Ironwood Creek was what her *Abuelo* Carlos called a service town, meaning it existed solely to support local industry—which in Ironwood Creek happened to be cattle and agriculture. Besides Jake and the deputy chief, Elena shared duties with two others. Not much ever happened of consequence, and protocol leaned toward lax. A hundred-and-eighty degrees from Elena's last position in Phoenix.

Sage Blackwell answered with her usual even tone. "How was the ever-congenial cat lady?"

"Let Jake know she may be calling him to report her dissatisfaction with me. Over."

"He'll love that." Sage had been the station secretary and deputy chief's assistant for the past three years. Nothing fazed her.

"Maybe you can run interference? Over."

"I'll try. Can't promise."

Elena nodded to herself. She liked Jake. He was the only member of the station's informal boys' club to treat Elena like an actual deputy and not Sage's underling, good only for brewing coffee, answering the phone and dealing with nuisance calls. Not that he'd taken Elena under his wing. He had a reputation to maintain with his buddies, after all. But at least he talked to her with respect and, when no one was listening, offered advice.

"Thanks. I'm going to patrol behind the abandoned pecan orchard. See you at the station in about an hour. Over and out."

"Be careful." Sage recited those two words every time and

to everyone when she signed off. In that regard, Elena was an accepted member of the team.

Patrolling the abandoned orchard had been the first duty assigned to her when she arrived in Ironwood Creek. Grunt work for the untested rookie considered to be a liability in the field. Elena wasn't sent on calls to investigate stolen cattle or defuse a domestic situation. She didn't bust drug dealers or even break up bar fights.

Instead, she helped tourists move their disabled vehicles from blocking traffic, picked up homeless individuals in the park and drove them to the shelter, and responded to irate older women with fat cats who didn't get along with their neighbors. On occasion, and when no one else was available, she was called for backup. Like the time an enraged man had held his ex-girlfriend hostage in his parents' barn.

Incidents like that, however, were few and far between. Whether because she was new or a woman or both, Elena's fellow deputies and the chief didn't trust her. And neither had they given her the opportunity to prove herself. Yet.

The ancient pecan trees came into view, the late-afternoon sun glinting through their spindly barren branches. According to Sage, the orchard had been abandoned a decade ago and, to this day, the land remained tied up in a family trust, going unsold and untended. It had become a favorite party spot for errant teens. Not to mention a hideout for runaways and a magnet for stray dogs.

Elena's second pass revealed nothing more troublesome than a small herd of deer in search of grass, sparse in colder weather. At her appearance, they bounded away and vanished among the trees. She was just executing a U-turn when Sage's voice hailed her on the radio. Elena pressed the button on the transmitter.

"Deputy Tomes here." She always identified herself. Her protocol wasn't that lax. "What's up, Sage? Over."

"Chief needs you to head to Ridge Burnham's place. You know where that is?"

"I do. What's going on?"

"He called in. Found an old handgun buried under his well house."

All right. Not exactly a hostage situation, but more exciting than scaring away deer. Elena decided Oscar Wentworth, the other deputy on duty, must be busy. Otherwise, the chief would have sent him.

"I'll radio in when I arrive. Over and out."

"Be careful."

Elena knew Ridge Burnham, or more accurately, she was acquainted with him. He attended Hillside Church, the church home Elena had found since coming to Ironwood Creek. They'd met a few times through Jake, who also attended Hillside Church with his family. Jake was married to Ridge's older sister, Gracie. They had two adorable daughters, aged three and six.

That was another reason Elena thought Jake secretly helped her. Women like Elena were paving the way for little girls like his, showing them by example that they had no limits and could be whatever they wanted.

Five miles down the road, she turned into the Burnham place. A long dirt drive flanked by mesquite trees and the town's namesake ironwoods took her to the main house. She could imagine that a generation ago, the former cattle ranch had been a showplace. Now, it sat in disrepair, a victim of weather, neglect and vandalism. Jake once mentioned that Ridge had retired from a successful rodeo career with the intent of restoring the family ranch his late father had driven into the ground. From what Elena could see, he had his work cut out for him.

As she drew nearer to the house, she slowed. Ridge appeared from the doorway of a shed and waved her over. She pulled up next to an ATV and parked. Adjusting her cap and aviator sunglasses, she got out and started toward him.

"Afternoon, Ridge."

"Thanks for coming so quickly."

He took off his leather work gloves and stuffed them in the pockets of his fleece-lined jacket. When they shook hands, her slim fingers disappeared inside his larger, stronger ones. The sensation wasn't entirely unpleasant, but Elena instantly dismissed it. If she was interested in dating, Ridge's handsome features would appeal to her. But her career came first, and that wouldn't change until she'd established herself.

"I'm told you found an old handgun," she said.

"Yeah." He led her to the back of the ATV. "The main pipe in my well house has a leak. I was digging under the side of the well house when my shovel hit something that shouldn't have been there." He reached into the ATV's small bed and lifted a burlap cloth. There lay a .40 caliber revolver coated in dirt. "I found this."

Elena leaned closer. A Smith & Wesson, she thought, though that would need to be confirmed. "You should have left it there and waited for the professionals. It might have accidentally discharged."

"The gun's not loaded."

"You checked?"

"I did."

Elena had learned since coming to Ironwood Creek that most of the ranchers in the area were knowledgeable about firearms. The difference between rural and urban living.

"You're fortunate," she said. "Had the gun been loaded, you might not be standing here."

"I guess God was watching out for me."

"He was," Elena agreed. "I'm assuming you don't recognize the gun, or you wouldn't have called."

"I've never seen it before."

"Okay. I can take it to the station for you."

"And then what?" Ridge wasn't wearing sunglasses, and his intense blue eyes bored into hers.

"The serial number will be traced. Hopefully, we'll find the owner of record. Learn if the gun was reported stolen or used in a crime."

"The serial number's been ground off."

"You checked that, too?"

Rather than answer, Ridge asked, "Am I required by law to turn the gun over to you?"

"Is there a reason you wouldn't? You did call."

"I think it might have something to do with my dad's homicide."

"Ah." Elena had heard about the late Pete Burnham's murder eighteen years ago. The case remained unsolved and ice-cold.

"I don't want the gun to get buried at the bottom of some box in the evidence room or sent off to a lab, never to return."

He sounded like he was speaking from experience.

"Why do you think the gun's connected to your dad's homicide?"

"Because of this." Ridge removed more of the burlap cloth to reveal a rusty metal strongbox. Beside it lay a pair of bolt cutters and a padlock, the shackle split in two pieces. "Take a look."

He lifted the strongbox lid. Inside were neat stacks of what appeared to be banded hundred-dollar bills, each securely wrapped in plastic.

Elena felt her jaw go slack. "Huh."

"I found the strongbox after I called the station," Ridge said.

"That's a lot of cash."

"My rough count, over forty thousand dollars."

And rather than keep the money for himself, he'd reported it to the authorities. *Interesting*, thought Elena.

"I'm convinced my dad was either killed for what's in this

strongbox," Ridge said, "or he hid it because he knew some-one was after him."

She retreated a step from the ATV, the gravity of his discovery sinking in. "I need to call for backup."

Ridge watched Elena as she rested an elbow on the hood of her SUV and talked into her radio. Deputy Tomes, he amended. She was here on business. He'd met her a few times at church and seen her once or twice around town. On those occasions, she'd been out of uniform. He'd had trouble imagining the petite, dark-haired beauty wielding a gun and taking down criminals. She'd seemed too delicate.

He didn't have that problem today. She exuded a confidence worthy of admiration.

Because she was new to town, she may not know all the details of his dad's homicide. That could come in handy for Ridge. Or work against him. It was too soon to tell and too early in their acquaintance.

If things were different, he'd remedy that and ask her out for coffee. But his focus was elsewhere. Specifically on rebuilding the ranch and restoring his family's good name. Both had been damaged by his late father, and solving his homicide could help significantly with the latter.

Besides, Elena gave off strong not-interested-in-dating vibes. Ridge didn't take the slight personally. She gave off the same vibes to every unattached man who attempted to flirt with her, leastwise according to his sister, Gracie. As the church's self-appointed matchmaker, she'd know and would have moved mountains to put an attractive, available single woman like Elena in Ridge's path. Since he'd retired from the professional rodeo circuit and returned home, she'd made it her personal mission to find his soulmate.

Ridge wanted that, too. Someday. Just not yet.

Elena finished her radio call and returned to where Ridge waited by the ATV.

"Chief Dempsey will be here shortly. He's stopping to pick up Jake first."

Ridge nodded. He'd rather the chief came alone. Not that he didn't get along with his brother-in-law—Jake was a good husband to Ridge's sister, Gracie and a loving father. He and Ridge were fans of the same sports teams and enjoyed nothing better than riding the mountain trails surrounding Ironwood Creek. But they didn't agree when it came to Ridge's late father. Jake thought Ridge should leave the past in the past and move on with his life. In Jake's opinion, Pete Burnham had been a drunk and a good-for-nothing and undeserving of the effort and emotion Ridge expended on him.

"Would you like a water?" he asked Elena.

"Thank you."

"Come on inside. We'll be able to see when the chief and Jake arrive through the kitchen window."

Elena followed him to the rectangular courtyard at the rear of the house. Three citrus trees—a lemon, an orange, and a grapefruit—stood guard. This time of year, like every February, they were still heavy with fruit.

Ridge opened the wooden gate and motioned for her to precede him. He did the same at the door leading to the kitchen. Warm air enveloped them, a welcome relief from the forty-degree temperature outside.

"Make yourself comfortable." He indicated the kitchen table and then continued toward an ice chest on the floor, where he removed two bottles of water. Returning to the table, he handed a bottle to Elena.

She perched on the edge of the seat, every muscle rigid. When she removed her sunglasses, her large brown eyes met his gaze before traveling the room and noting every detail.

"You're remodeling," she said matter-of-factly.

Ridge hung his cowboy hat and jacket on the back of his chair before sitting across from her. "One of my many projects."

"Must be hard to fix meals with no appliances and no cabinets."

"I eat a lot of fast food. There's also a microwave and toaster oven on the TV tray over there." He unscrewed his bottled water and took a long swig. "The new cabinets will be installed the first of the week. The appliances after that."

"Should look nice."

"I'm limiting the inside work to the kitchen and bathrooms. For now. Most of my repairs and restorations will be to the outbuildings and grounds, which, I'm sure you noticed on your way in, are in bad shape."

"Like the well house?"

"Like the well house."

Elena considered for a moment. "What makes you think your father is the one who buried the gun and the money? Could have been anyone."

"Well, it wasn't my mom. That's for sure."

"You asked her?"

"No need. She'd have dug up the money years ago if she knew about it and kept every dime."

Ridge's mother shared Jake's low opinion of her late husband and disagreed with Ridge's efforts to rebuild the ranch, constantly pestering him to sell. Ridge refused. Pete Burnham had inherited the ranch from Ridge's grandfather and passed it on to his children. For now, Gracie supported Ridge's plans to renovate. That could change. Their mom pestered Gracie, too.

"My sister and I were young when Dad died," he said. "Who else but him could have, or would have, buried the gun and strongbox?"

Elena sipped her water. "Let's assume for a minute it was your dad. How did he come into such a large sum of money? I heard he…didn't work much."

"That's true." Ridge tried to ignore the eighteen-year-old ache in his chest. "Worse than that, he drank away most of what little money he did earn. So, no, I have no idea how he acquired forty thousand dollars. Except my gut tells me he's the one who buried it there. If a cartel drug runner needed a place to hide money and a gun, they'd have buried it in the mountains, not beneath someone's well house where the owner might find it."

Elena sat up. "Drug runner?"

"Didn't anyone tell you when you took the job?"

"Tell me what?"

"Ironwood Creek has a pretty unsavory history."

"Really?"

"Look it up. We used to be a gateway town for bringing illegal drugs into the country. At night, you could see headlights winding through the outskirts of town. I used to watch them from my bedroom window traveling the far edges of our ranch. When I asked my mom about the headlights, she told me I was imagining things. My dad said to just ignore them and go to sleep."

"What was done to stop the drug runners?"

"Nothing. People bolted their doors and stayed inside."

Elena shook her head. "I had no idea."

"An altercation with a drug runner is the explanation we were given for my dad's homicide. He must have encountered one of them, who then pushed him off the ledge into the ravine. Evidence at the scene pointed to a possible struggle."

Elena studied Ridge thoughtfully. "But you don't believe that story."

"Not for a minute."

"Why?"

Her talents were being wasted as a deputy. She'd make a fine investigator. Not only because she asked questions, but because she listened and observed.

"Earlier on the day my dad was killed, I went out to the barn looking for him. When I got there, I heard him arguing with some guy. I was curious and a little scared. My dad seldom raised his voice. I ducked around the side of the barn and snuck in the back entrance. I hid behind the tractor and eaves-dropped. They were too busy yelling to notice me."

"What were they arguing about?"

"Someone named the Hawk who was on the way. My dad apparently had an agreement with them."

"Them being the Hawk?" Elena asked.

"I'm not sure. Not much of what they said made sense."

"What else?"

"The guy kept saying my dad gave his word and going back on it would cost him and his family. That's when the two of them got into a scuffle. Next thing, the guy shoved my dad to the ground, told him that he was a dead man and stormed out. I ran to my dad and helped him up. He insisted he was okay, that it was nothing, and not to tell my mom."

"Did you describe this man to the authorities?"

Ridge snorted in disgust. "For all the good it did. Long hair. Scruffy beard. A brown T-shirt and jeans. I might have been describing any random fifty guys in Ironwood Creek. The detective said it didn't matter, anyway. I was young and, according to him, an unreliable witness."

"How old were you?"

"Twelve. Almost thirteen."

"Not that young," Elena commented.

She was the first person to agree with Ridge.

"My age was irrelevant," he said. "People were determined to discredit me."

"What people?"

"I don't know. Maybe those who stood to benefit the most from the mass amounts of illegal drugs being moved through the area. Millions of dollars' worth. Operations that size don't exist without help and without law enforcement and elected officials turning a blind eye. For a percentage, I'm sure. Isn't that how these things work?"

"That's a serious accusation. Do you have anything to back it up?"

"Only suspicions." He shrugged and took another swig of water. "Which, I've learned, will get you nowhere."

"You think your dad was involved with the cartel?"

"Involved or a witness." Ridge leaned forward. "My dad wasn't the only one killed. See for yourself. Find his case and read about it."

Elena also leaned forward. "Do you suspect the man your dad argued with killed him?"

"Yes."

"What evidence at the scene made the police rule your dad's death a homicide?"

"Footprints and broken branches, plus the location and position of my dad's body, all indicated he'd been pushed. Nothing to identify who did the pushing. No game or security cameras. No witness driving by."

"Unfortunately, that's not uncommon."

"But I found something in the barn that day," Ridge continued. "On the ground, in the dirt. A gold chain. It must have belonged to the guy and fell off when he and my dad scuffled. When I showed the chain to my dad, he ripped it out of my hands and shoved it in his pocket." Ridge swallowed what felt like a tangle of barbed wire. "Five hours later he was dead, and the gold chain wasn't in his pocket."

"You think he hid the chain or that whoever might have pushed him took it?"

"My guess is he hid it."

"Why?"

"Insurance. To use against the guy he argued with."

Elena released a long breath. "I wish I could say differently, Ridge, but that doesn't prove anything."

"If I can find the chain, it might. My dad didn't leave after the scuffle, and no one else came over. It wasn't until later, near dusk, that he hiked into the hills. Since the chain wasn't on him, and he didn't give it to any of us, it must be somewhere on this ranch."

"What if he disposed of it?"

"I went through the trash. I wanted to show the police I wasn't inventing stories for attention."

Anger and frustration rose anew and clawed to the surface. He heard again the accusations made by thoughtless individuals that had shaped his future life, almost as much as losing his father at a young age had. Years of riding bulls and broncs hadn't driven away the pain. Neither had prayer, nor counseling from his Cowboy Church preacher. He hoped restoring the ranch would finally bring him peace.

Perhaps his brother-in-law was right and Ridge needed to let go of the past—but he wasn't ready. And finding the gun and money felt like a sign from above for him to continue seeking answers.

"Why did your dad hike up into the hills?" Elena asked. "Seems a strange thing to do so late in the day."

"Not that strange." One of the fond memories Ridge had of his dad returned. Too often, it felt like he was the only one who remembered the late Pete Burnham with affection. "He was an amateur prospector. We went out together a lot. Never found much to brag about, but we had fun. That's what counts."

"Was any prospecting equipment found at the scene of the homicide?" Elena asked.

"None."

"Okay. So, if he didn't go into the hills to prospect, then why?"

"To meet the Hawk?" Ridge suggested.

"Or to get away from him."

He sat up, suddenly energized. Why hadn't he considered that before? After the argument with the bearded guy, Ridge should have realized his dad had been running from danger.

The next instant, a different, more alarming scenario occurred to him.

"Dad could have been drawing his killer away from the

ranch. To save me, my sister and my mom. The guy he'd been arguing with did threaten the family."

"That's possible," Elena agreed. "But unfortunately, you'll probably never know."

For the first time, emotion showed in her expression. Ridge saw compassion and empathy mixed with sorrow and felt a sudden bond with her. Perhaps, like him, she'd suffered loss and had failed to receive needed closure.

Before he could respond, they heard the rumble of an approaching vehicle. Ridge pushed back from the table and stood. Elena followed suit, and they both glanced out the kitchen window.

"The chief and Jake are here," he said, and reached for his cowboy hat and jacket.

She put on her sunglasses and followed him outside. Ridge readied himself for what would no doubt be yet another battle with law enforcement.

TWO

Ridge watched Elena from the corner of his eye as they strode to where Chief Dempsey had parked his SUV next to hers. If this were a social call, Ridge supposed his brother-in-law would have clapped him on the back. Instead, Jake and the chief made straight for Elena, giving Ridge no more than a cursory nod and brusque "Hello."

"This way," she said and motioned for them to accompany her. "The gun and strongbox are in the back of the ATV."

The four of them formed a semicircle and stared wordlessly into the bed. Chief Dempsey removed a pair of disposal blue gloves from his pocket and slipped them on, tugging the ends for a tight fit. They were the kind of gloves Ridge had seen used by lab techs and nurses.

Only when the chief was satisfied did he lift the lid on the strongbox. "Would you look at that?"

Jake moved in closer and emitted a low whistle. "Hoo, doggie."

With his damp hair, he looked like he'd showered and dressed minutes before being fetched by the chief. Likely true as he'd pulled the graveyard shift this week. Ridge was certain the chief had brought Jake along only because he and Ridge were related by marriage, and Jake might "talk some sense" into Ridge.

A similar talk had happened once before when Ridge returned home six months ago and insisted he be given access to old mugshots—his goal being to see if he recognized the guy his dad had been arguing with in the barn. He'd been denied, and Jake was called in. Ridge had wanted Jake to go to bat for him. When he refused, the brothers-in-law hadn't watched football together for weeks. A birthday party for one of Ridge's nieces had provided the opportunity both were seeking to set aside their differences.

"Jake." The chief hitched his chin at his SUV. "Grab a couple evidence bags, will ya?"

"Yes, sir." He hurried off.

"What are you going to do?" Ridge asked the chief.

The silver-haired man paused to assess him. Despite his short, stocky frame, he exuded a sense of power and authority that garnered law-abiding citizens' respect and intimidated lawbreakers.

"What would you like me to do?"

Ridge didn't miss a beat. "Reopen my dad's homicide."

"The case isn't closed."

"No one's investigated it for years."

"There's been no new leads."

"Until today."

The chief grunted, his gaze cutting from the strongbox to Ridge. "Nothing to indicate this gun and money are related to your dad's death."

"His murder."

"That hasn't been fully established. Could have been an accident or self-defense."

Ridge gritted his teeth. Condescending tones had that effect on him. "Then why didn't the person turn themself in?"

Jake had returned by then. "Come on, Ridge. Give it a rest, okay? We're not going to solve what happened to your dad today."

"We might. If the chief sends these items in for testing."

"What do you think they'll find?" the chief asked, opening the first evidence bag.

"Fingerprints or DNA. My dad's. His murderer's. Both."

"These items look to have been buried a long time ago. Evidence degrades." The chief placed the gun inside the bag and sealed it. "You said you found these by your well house pipe. There'll be water damage."

"Have the items tested, Chief."

"Be reasonable, Ridge," Jake cajoled. "We'd be wasting taxpayers' money."

Ridge refused to back down. Not this time. "Drug runners transported their product across our ranch. That's a fact. My dad, who may or may not have been on the take, was killed. That's also a fact. A gun and money were buried beneath my well house. You can't convince me the three aren't connected."

Only Elena looked as if she believed him. The chief and Jake exchanged here-we-go-again glances. Ridge tamped down his rising temper.

"My dad may not have been a model citizen or father of the year, but he never hurt anybody in his life and didn't have a mean bone in his body. He didn't deserve to be pushed off that ledge and left for the turkey vultures."

That was how the search party had found Ridge's dad two days after he'd gone missing: vultures circling in the sky above the hills.

"No, you're right," the chief agreed, dialing his gruffness down a notch. "I understand your need for answers."

"Then you'll test the gun and the strongbox?"

He nodded and placed the strongbox into the second evidence bag. "I'll send them to the lab tomorrow."

Ridge took what felt like his first real breath since finding the gun. "Thank you."

"No promises on what they'll find. And the results could take some time."

"Any chance you can expedite the request?"

The chief furrowed his brow, his authoritative demeanor back in full force. "Don't push it."

"What about the money?" Jake asked. "What happens to it, assuming the tests come back inconclusive? Can Ridge make a claim?"

"You'll have to check into that, Ridge," the chief said. "There's a procedure. Paperwork to be filed."

Jake grinned. "Wait till Gracie hears."

Ridge's sister. Naturally, she'd be entitled to half of anything found on the ranch that they were allowed to keep, and Ridge would see that she got her fair share.

The chief carried the evidence bag containing the strongbox to his SUV. Jake trailed behind him with the bagged gun. They secured the items on the floor of the rear seat. When the chief shut the door and turned, Ridge was waiting for him.

"Mind if I call you in a couple of days?" he asked.

The chief frowned. "I'll call you."

"You need my number?"

"Jake has it."

Ridge's brother-in-law did clap him on the shoulder then in a show of forced camaraderie. "Relax, buddy. Don't get yourself tied in a knot."

He caught Elena's mildly exasperated glance—aimed at Jake. The earlier bond he'd felt with her grew. He really liked Ironwood Creek's newest deputy sheriff.

"Let's go, Jake," the chief said and ambled toward the driver's-side door as if in no hurry at all.

Regardless of what he said to the contrary, Ridge knew in that instant that the chief would put little weight on his discovery. What else was new?

"Deputy Tomes?" the chief called over his shoulder. "You coming?"

"Yes, sir. I mean, I'll be along shortly." She stood taller, an accomplishment considering the top of her head barely reached

Ridge's chin. "I thought I might have Ridge show me the well house so I can take a few pictures. For my report."

"Look at you," Jake singsonged. "The rookie deputy covering all the bases."

Ridge sensed Elena stiffen.

"Don't be too long," the chief said.

"No, sir. I won't."

The chief and Jake climbed in and drove away, the vehicle's rear wheels sending twin plumes of red dust into the chilly afternoon air.

Ridge shoved his hands into his jacket pockets and stared after the SUV, his thoughts too tangled to sort. *Please, Lord, let this discovery help reveal the answers I seek.*

"Ridge?"

Rousing himself, he faced Elena. "Yeah. Sorry."

"Do you mind taking me to the well house? If you have somewhere else to be—"

"I don't mind. Anything to move the investigation along."

She smiled. Not much, just a slight lifting at the corners of her mouth. He imagined the reserved deputy's face alight with joy. That, he supposed, would be a sight to see, if an unlikely one. Which was a shame. She had nice eyes, and it was too bad she always hid them behind those sunglasses.

The two of them walked side by side through the barn, empty of livestock for almost two decades now. Birds flitted between the rafters, annoyed their tranquility had been disturbed. Once, the Burnhams had owned an old horse, a couple of nanny goats and a flock of chickens. Ridge's mom had sold eggs and goat's milk to bring in extra money. Ridge and his sister looked after the animals, as well as tended the vegetable garden behind the house.

During lean times, when Ridge's dad wasn't working or when he drank up his weekly wages, they'd survived on corn and squash and eggs and the kindness of friends. Ridge had learned at a young age how to pasteurize goat's milk, which they drank themselves when that was all they had. To this day, he hated it.

He and Elena passed by the ancient tractor Ridge had hidden behind on the day his dad argued with the bearded stranger. It hadn't run then and still didn't. One of these days, Ridge would haul it to the junkyard.

Reaching the back of the barn, he slid open a latch and threw wide the door, the hinges protesting from lack of use.

"Guess I need to grease those," he said.

Elena stepped outside. "How far is the well house?"

"At the top of that rise." He pointed to a small, square structure. "My granddad built the well on high ground. Gravity carries the water to the barn and house by an underground pipe."

"The well is wind powered." Elena nodded at the tall tower beside the well house with a spinning windmill on top. "Very eco-friendly."

"And less expensive than electricity."

They trudged up the rise. The wind increased the higher they went, stinging their faces and forcing them to hold their hats to their heads.

He took her around the backside of the well house to the hole he'd dug. Water dripped from where he'd taped the leak before going down to meet Elena. His shovel, pick and other equipment lay scattered on the ground where he'd left them, along with a toolbox.

Elena began snapping pictures with her phone from different angles.

"Don't take this question the wrong way," Ridge said, "but would you mind calling me tomorrow and letting me know the chief shipped off the gun and money for testing?"

She paused, her demeanor guarded. "If you're worried he won't—"

Ridge cut her short. "I am worried."

Her chin tilted up a notch. "I don't appreciate what you're implying. The chief is a public servant sworn to uphold the law."

"My dad's homicide was swept under the carpet, and the case has been left to rot for eighteen years."

"Ridge." She paused as if mentally counting to ten. "You were young when your dad died, right? And then you left town five years later, returning only occasionally. You may not have the clearest, most unbiased recollection of events."

"Are you done taking pictures?"

"Almost."

She snapped several close-ups of the hole.

Their return walk to the house was in uncomfortable silence. At her SUV, Elena opened the driver's-side door and sat, filling out paperwork.

"If I need additional information," she said, "I'll contact you."

"I'm sorry if I offended you, Elena."

"You didn't."

"Your boss, then."

She filled out a small white card. Emerging from the SUV, she handed him the card. "Here's the incident number, in case you need it."

He glanced down, noting she'd included her name and badge number as well. "Thanks."

And then she was gone. Ridge watched her taillights growing smaller and smaller and wanted to kick himself. He'd hoped to find an ally in Elena. Any possibility of that was now ruined, thanks to him and his inability to keep his opinions to himself.

She wasn't going to read up on Ironwood Creek's history or confirm the chief sent the gun and money to Tucson for testing. In fact, he'd be surprised if she ever talked to him again.

Elena sat at one of the two desks occupying the station's central room, her eyes glued to the computer screen as she clicked through pages. Jake had been at the other desk when she first returned from the Burnham ranch but was currently out on a call. A guest at the Creekside Inn had reported their car broken into and expensive photography equipment stolen.

Just as well he wasn't here. Elena was still a little annoyed with him. His remark about her being a rookie deputy had stung. Jake normally treated her with more respect than that. She wondered if he'd felt he had an image to uphold in front of the chief or Ridge. Maybe both. Frankly, she had little use for people who tried to make themselves appear superior by putting others down.

Shaking off the irritation, she continued reading and was soon engrossed. So much so, she didn't notice Sage Blackwater until the station secretary was standing behind her and peering over her shoulder.

"I thought you were off duty a half hour ago," she said.

"I was." It was too late for Elena to minimize the screen. "Just finishing some paperwork."

"That doesn't look like a report on the cat lady's complaint."

"It's not."

Sage leaned closer, her purse hanging from her shoulder and an empty reusable cup in her hand. When she arrived at the station tomorrow, the cup would be filled with a green power smoothie. "Isn't that the police report on Pete Burnham's death?"

Having been busted, Elena chose to come clean. "I thought I might read up on him. In case something comes of the discovery at the ranch today."

"Hmm."

"You know anything about what happened to him?"

Sage straightened and smoothed her long black ponytail with her free hand. "That was way before my time here."

"But you've lived in Ironwood Creek your whole life. There must have been talk."

"I was taking classes at Cochise College and working part-time when Pete died. I didn't pay much attention to local happenings. Too busy."

"A homicide is a big deal." Elena had the distinct impression Sage knew far more than she was willing to reveal.

"I can tell you this," the secretary admitted. "I remember my parents arguing. With each other and friends. Apparently, the whole town was divided. Half the people believed Pete was a drunk and a loser and had probably fallen to his death regardless of the evidence at the scene. His wife included."

"That must have been hard on Ridge and his sister."

"I don't know them well. I've met Gracie a few times through Jake, and Ridge because of his dealings with the station. But I can imagine being the subject of gossip for your entire life must be hard. I'm told Ridge idolized his dad." She sighed. "Children can be naive. They don't see their parents' faults."

Elena pictured Ridge as a twelve-year-old, losing the dad he loved. Hopefully, restoring his family's ranch would help him heal, whether his dad's homicide case remained stalled or was eventually solved.

"What about the town's other half?" she asked Sage.

"They were upset and afraid."

"Because a killer was on the loose?"

"No one was sure the deaths were accidental or intentional. And if intentional, then…"

"Deaths?" Elena's interest sparked. "As in plural?"

"There were other unsolved homicides over the years."

"Related to the drug trafficking?"

The typically unflappable station secretary reacted, her glance cutting to the door. "That was never proven one way or the other."

Ridge had been right. Ironwood Creek did have an ugly history. And a scary one.

"How many?" Elena asked.

"Two, other than Pete Burnham."

"When did they occur?"

Sage hedged. "The first one twenty-two, twenty-three years

ago. Then Pete. The last one about eight years ago. It was just before Sheriff Cochrane was elected and implemented his crack-down-on-crime program."

The same sheriff whose participation with the governor's new hiring program was responsible for Elena landing the job at Ironwood Creek.

"Not that our problems were the county's worst ones," Sage hastily added. "Crime rates in Benson and Sierra Vista were soaring then, too."

"Tell me about the other murders," Elena said, circling back to their original topic. "Who were the victims, and what happened to them?"

"Sorry. Can't. I have to go." Sage retreated a step. "I'll be late picking up the kids from basketball practice. See you tomorrow."

"Have a good evening."

She all but fled, leaving Elena alone. The chief had already gone home for the day, and Jake hadn't returned from the inn. Elena used the opportunity to sidle over to Sage's desk and check out the shipping boxes the secretary had packed earlier. Per the printed labels, they were headed to the forensic crime laboratory in Tucson.

The chief had kept his promise to Ridge. Elena reconsidered calling him as he'd requested. After reading the report on his dad's homicide and talking to Sage, she found she'd softened toward him.

Not that Elena had much experience with homicides—all right, almost none. In Phoenix, where she was from, deputy sheriffs didn't investigate homicides. That job fell to local police. But even to her novice eye, this report lacked details. As if the investigating detective, a Frank Darnelly out of Bisbee, had exerted only the most minimal effort required.

Ridge's accounting of his dad's argument with the stranger in the barn wasn't even included. In the detective's defense, no proof existed the stranger had been involved in Pete Burnham's death. Nonetheless, the incident was noteworthy and should have been included in the witnesses' reports. It certainly established motive. Someone had been angry at Pete Burnham and threatened him and his family.

Printing out a copy of the police report, Elena folded the papers in half and carried them to the breakroom in the rear of the station. There, she keyed in the combination on her locker, retrieved her backpack and stuck the papers inside.

Taking a copy of the report wasn't illegal or even against policy. She could justify her actions as background research on the gun and money discovery. But she'd rather no one knew. She took plenty of grief from her fellow deputies as it was. They were bound to criticize her interest in the case and poke fun at her rather than commend her for being thorough.

Returning to the central room, she paused. She could lock up, arm the security system and leave. The place wouldn't be empty for long—Jake would be returning soon. He'd only come on duty early in order to accompany the chief to the Burnham ranch. Why, Elena couldn't be sure. Her first thought had been because the chief didn't trust her, but after seeing Jake and Ridge together, she wondered if there was another, entirely personal reason. More than Ridge's frustration with the lack of interest in reinvestigating his father's homicide.

Rather than head home, Elena returned to her desk and resumed her research, looking online for information about Pete Burnham. There wasn't much. A few brief newspaper articles revealing little more than she'd already learned and an obituary. Exhausting that avenue, she accessed the sheriff's department records archives available to her. There, she had a bit more success.

Pete Burnham had been arrested four times on petty charges. Public intoxication, disturbing the peace, trespassing and shoplifting. That last charge appeared to be more of a misunderstanding. He'd walked out of a convenience store with a bag of chips and a beer, claiming he thought he'd paid for them. Considering he went no further than the curb where he sat down to eat the chips and drink the beer, Elena tended to believe his claim.

He'd had enough money on him and offered to pay for the items, but the store owner insisted on pressing charges. They'd wanted to discourage Pete from ever darkening the market's door again. Apparently, he was a regular customer and a regular troublemaker. Loud. Pestering the other customers. Loitering. His mugshot showed a happy, disheveled drunk.

If Pete Burnham had any juvenile offenses, those records were sealed. Elena assumed there were none, since his offenses and apparent penchant for public drinking didn't appear to start until he was in his mid-twenties. If he drank before then, he'd managed to control himself and avoid trouble. What had changed for him? A quick side search revealed he'd gotten married about then, and Ridge's sister was born a few months later. A coincidence? Were the pressures of marriage and parenthood too much for him?

Elena did another search on crime in Ironwood Creek. Here, the results were mixed. There was a lot of it, no question. But again, sparse on details. Most of the articles and opinion pieces appeared in newspapers outside the immediate area. Sierra Vista. Tucson. Phoenix. Ironwood Creek had made the list of Arizona's top-five towns with the highest crime rates for a dozen straight years. And yet, from what Ridge had said, no one ever did anything about it until Sheriff Cochrane came along.

The sudden opening of the station door gave her a start.

"Hey. What are you doing here?"

This time, Elena acted fast and clicked out of the page she'd been viewing. "Hi, Jake. Just finishing up. About ready to hit the road."

By the time the sergeant deputy came around to her side of the desk, the computer screen was blank save for the sign-in screen. Elena released a quiet sigh of relief.

"Everything go okay at the inn?" she asked, grabbing her backpack and standing.

"What a mess. I mean, who leaves five-thousand-dollars' worth of photography equipment in their vehicle? He was practically begging to be robbed. Don't tourists realize burglars constantly case hotels looking for easy marks?"

"That's a shame."

"What's a shame is that he tried blaming the inn. Then went ballistic when the manager pointed out the small print on the agreement he signed stating the inn isn't responsible for items left in vehicles parked on the premises."

"Was there any security footage?"

"Didn't reveal much. The perps, two of them, were wearing hoodies and ski masks. They knew what they were doing. In and out of the car in less than five minutes."

"I hope his equipment was insured."

"He was on the phone with his insurance agent when I pulled out."

"That's good." Elena gave Jake a half smile. "See you tomorrow?"

"Yeah, but…" He grinned sheepishly. "If you got a sec. I'm glad I caught you, actually. I sort of wanted to clear the air."

"Oh? About what?"

He removed his ball cap and tossed it onto the desk across from hers. "What I said earlier at Ridge's. About you being a rookie and covering all the bases."

She waited in silence for him to continue, not making it easy for him.

"You were doing a good job." He cleared his throat. "I was out of line."

"Did you tell that to the chief? Or Ridge?"

"What?" He chuckled, only to sober. "Seriously? Come on, Elena."

"Is that all? Because I'm getting hungry."

"Don't be mad."

"I think I have good reason. At Ridge's, you implied I'm inexperienced in front of our superior and the victim. But now, when no one's around to hear, you tell me I'm doing a good job. Which is it, Jake?"

He had the decency to blush. "You're the first female deputy any of us has had to work with. Ever. And you're just a kid, for crying out loud. You have to expect to take a little ribbing."

"How old were you when you started here?"

"Twenty-six. Fresh out of police academy."

"I'm twenty-eight."

"No fooling?" His dark brows shot up. "Cuz you look—"

She held out her hand in warning. "Don't say it."

"Okay, okay." He rocked back on his heels and patted his belly where it hung slightly over his belt. He wasn't out of shape, but Jake had the appearance of someone who never missed a meal. He liked to brag he knew his way around the backyard barbecue, and his smoked ribs were the best in town. "Just give us a little more time, okay? We're not a bad bunch."

"All right. Apology accepted."

"Good girl."

Elena stiffened. "Girl?"

"Oops. My bad. I've got daughters. It slipped out. Forgive me."

"Fine. On one condition." Elena went out on a limb. "You answer a couple questions for me."

"What kind of questions?"

"Tell me about the drug trafficking that used to go on here. You were a deputy then."

He frowned. "Why do you want to know that?"

"Because Pete Burnham's death may be related."

"You've been listening to Ridge."

"It makes sense."

"What, that a drug runner killed Pete? You'll get no disagreement from me. And I reckon one of them could've buried the gun and the money. It sure wasn't Pete. A drug runner is the only reasonable explanation. But if you're trying to tie Pete's homicide to the gun and money Ridge found…" Jake chuckled. "That's a stretch. A mighty big one."

"People have been killed for less than forty thousand dollars."

"Pete was killed because he saw something he shouldn't have seen or could identify someone who didn't want to be identified."

"Like the Hawk?"

"The what?"

"Never mind." Elena changed tactics. "It'll be interesting to see the test results on the gun and money."

Jake glanced over at Sage's desk and then snorted in disgust. "Nothing's gonna come of that. Those things have been in the ground too long."

"The chief must think it's worth checking into. He's sending them to Tucson."

"Don't be so sure. He's just going through the motions. Easier that way. Ridge can make problems for him otherwise."

"He doesn't strike me as the type."

"Oh, he's the type. Likes to call the county sheriff's office and complain."

"He's searching for answers."

"Don't get swept up. I'm warning you, Elena."

"Warning me?"

"Yes, I am." Jake's features darkened. "I was here when the cartel reigned king. They wielded their power over the entire town, and everyone in it. No one was safe. If Pete Burnham was involved with them, and I'm not convinced he was, he died because he made the wrong person mad."

"What are you saying, Jake?"

"Ridge is going to find himself in the same position as his dad if he's not careful. And you, too, Elena, if you insist on getting involved."

"We have a duty to investigate Pete Burnham's death."

"The cartel has never showed mercy. And they don't forget. They may have gone underground, but they're not gone. That's why I want Ridge to quit stirring the pot. Not because he's wasting his time. Because I'd hate for my wife to lose her brother as well as her father."

Jake's comment stayed with Elena all that evening. But rather than scare her off, it convinced her she needed to speak to the chief at the first opportunity. He was the only one at the station who could, and possibly would, willingly answer her questions.

THREE

Elena sat in the third pew from the back, her usual spot for Sunday morning worship service at Hillside Church. Funny how regulars had their favorite seats. Her family in Phoenix would arrive to their church with no less than six and sometimes as many as ten in their group. As a teen, she'd roll her eyes whenever her parents laid claim to "their row."

And now, here was Elena, just like them.

She smiled to herself. In only four months, she'd embraced life as a resident of Ironwood Creek—at least inasmuch as having her regular seat at church. All that remained was being accepted by her peers at work and making a few friends.

She'd been remiss with that last one, though who could blame her? Friendship required effort and time. She worked long, unmanageable hours. Hard to make plans with gal pals when her schedule changed one week to the next, and she might be called in on a moment's notice.

Not that she related well to other women when she did get together with them. They didn't like hearing about her job. Elena's sister called her a downer. A downer! She was in law enforcement. There was no cooler job on the planet.

Her sister also said Elena scared off potential friends. She intimidated them with her job and her no-nonsense attitude. Ridiculous. Elena wasn't no-nonsense. Levelheaded, yes. Pragmatic, perhaps. But those were good qualities.

Except, she apparently scared off men, too. If Elena believed her sister, they were attracted to her until they learned what she did for a living. She refused to accept that. If men were intimidated by her, it was because being married to someone in law enforcement wasn't easy for everyone. The job took a toll on relationships and families. As the daughter of a detective and granddaughter of a police sergeant, Elena could attest to that.

"Have a lovely day."

She blinked and discovered Mr. Harmon's smiling face at the end of her pew. "Same to you, sir."

She realized then that the sanctuary was nearly empty. Everyone had filed out at the end of the service—which was a good one. The minister's sermon had touched on the role of parents, and she found herself missing her own mom and dad. Her siblings, too. Her older sister and cousin were both expecting babies. Elena's mom had begun dropping hints to Elena about finding someone special and starting a family. She wasn't particularly keen on Elena following in her dad and grandfather's footsteps, citing the job's inherent danger.

At least Phoenix wasn't that far, a three-and-a-half-hour drive, so she visited monthly. Her family visited her, too. Elena's mom liked to fuss over Elena's small apartment and reorganize her cupboards. Her little brother and sister brought their swimsuits and workout clothes so they could use the apartment complex's trendy pool and gym. Her dad tuned up her car and engaged in cop talk. He was considering retiring in a year or two. Elena made enchiladas for everyone using her *abuela*'s recipe. The visits were always wonderful and filled her emotional well.

She made a mental note to call her mom when she got home.

Outside the sanctuary, several groups of people lingered in the foyer, chatting and laughing. Elena smiled and nodded, weaving her way toward the church's double glass doors.

"Elena. Hi," Olivia Gifford, the church bookkeeper, called. "Will you be joining us for coffee hour today?"

Beverages and sweets were served every Sunday after morning service in the fellowship hall. Elena usually ducked out, often because she had to work later that day or had worked all night and needed sleep. She started to tell Olivia no, only to remember her earlier thought about expanding her social circle.

"Sure. Sounds good."

"Great." Oliva brightened. "See you there."

Elena's flats echoed on the concrete walkway as she crossed from the sanctuary to the fellowship hall. She rarely wore dresses. Church was one of the few exceptions. Elena's mother had insisted, and the habit had stuck long past Elena moving out to attend college.

After graduating from the police academy, she'd considered joining the force like her dad and grandfather. A recruiter from the sheriff's department changed her mind. Amazing how a day, a plan, a life, could take a sudden and unexpected turn.

Kind of like spotting Ridge the moment she stepped into the fellowship hall. He sat at a table with his sister and Jake, and his nieces.

With his back to the door, he didn't see her, and she considered leaving. They hadn't spoken since their brief phone call when she'd told him the gun and strongbox had been shipped to the lab in Tucson. She'd intended that to be their last discussion. And while the idea of the gun and strongbox having something to do with Pete Burnham's death was intriguing, there was nothing concrete to connect it to Ironwood Creek's violent drug trafficking history.

And yet…

Her conversation yesterday with the chief had changed her opinion. As she'd listened to him, she found that some of Ridge's remarks that day at the ranch no longer seemed far-fetched. Elena wanted to tell Ridge about what she'd learned and help if she could. But not here and not now when he was surrounded by his family.

Granted, she should probably mind her own business. She wasn't a detective and felt unqualified to investigate an eighteen-year-old homicide. Moreover, the case didn't involve her, and she'd only get more flak from the chief and the other deputies. Not to mention Jake's concerns for her and Ridge's well-being if they kept poking into the drug cartel. But nothing about Pete Burnham's homicide added up, and Elena was having trouble ignoring the constant gnawing on her insides.

All at once, Ridge rose and headed toward the beverage table. He caught sight of her, and their gazes connected. Elena started forward. Neither of them looked away, not even when they were standing two feet apart.

"Morning, Ridge."

"Can I get you a coffee?" He held up an empty Styrofoam cup.

"Um…" Elena noticed people casting curious glances in their direction. Jake and Ridge's sister, Gracie, openly stared. "I was wondering if you had time to talk. About your dad's case."

"Now?"

"If you're free. I'm on duty later today."

"Absolutely." He indicated the room with a tilt of his head. "We can grab an empty table."

She shot a quick look at Jake and Gracie. "Have you had breakfast?"

"Just a stale donut before church. I was going to stop on the way home."

"More fast food?"

He smiled. "Guilty as charged."

"We could go to the Sunnyside Café." The nearby breakfast and lunch spot was a favorite of Elena's.

"Real food. How can I refuse?"

"Meet you there?"

"Let's go." He motioned toward the door.

"Do you need to talk to your family first?"

He chuckled. "I don't want to give my sister any ideas, particularly the wrong ones."

Elena thought they might be too late. From Gracie's hearts-in-her-eyes expression, she was entertaining all sorts of ideas.

Fifteen minutes later, Ridge met up with Elena at the café entrance. As expected for a Sunday morning, the place was packed, and they had to wait for a table.

"Apologies in advance if my sister corners you and gives you grief," he said.

"Grief? About what?"

They stood elbow to elbow with people on all sides and had to lean close in order to be heard above the din of clattering dishes and noisy conversations. Delicious aromas filled the air and caused Ridge's stomach to rumble.

"Gracie will jump to conclusions about us leaving church together."

"Oh." Elena gave Ridge a firm look. "But you'll set her straight."

"I'll do my best. My sister can be intentionally obtuse."

"How does she feel about your dad's homicide? Can I ask?"

Ridge took his time before answering. "She's older than me and saw more of Dad's drinking and the bad side of our parents' marriage. That's not to say she didn't love Dad and regret his death. She's just happier not dwelling on our miserable childhood and would rather I let the case lie."

"What did she say when she learned about the gun and the money?"

"She's mad I showed you the strongbox and wishes I'd split the money with her instead. Which I get. She's half owner of the ranch and feels I should have talked to her first. She and Jake have two daughters and can use twenty thousand dollars."

"You'll likely get the money back," Elena said.

"Hopefully. But you have to remember, she has Jake in her ear. And our mom. They all three want me to sell the ranch."

"I hope you turning in the gun and money doesn't drive a wedge between you and your family."

"It won't. At least I don't think it will," he said. "Even if Gracie and my mom don't always agree with me, they love me. And Jake loves Gracie. He'll go along with whatever she wants."

"I have to admit," Elena said, "I was surprised you turned the money in. You're renovating the ranch and could also use twenty thousand dollars."

He shrugged. "I did okay rodeoing."

"Five World titles, I heard."

"Something like that."

"Impressive. When did you retire?"

"About six months ago. Which is also when I began renovating the ranch. And pestering Chief Dempsey to reopen my dad's homicide."

Before he could say more, the hostess called out, "Table ready for the Burnham party."

Ridge touched Elena's shoulder and guided her past a family with teenagers. He meant nothing by the gesture. The space leading to the table for two tucked in a corner by the window was narrow. That was what he told himself, anyway.

A young man wearing a green apron appeared and held up a thermal carafe. "Coffee?"

"Please." Ridge pushed his mug forward, and the young man poured.

"Do you have any herbal tea?" Elena asked.

"Be right back."

"Tea?" Ridge asked after their server left. "I thought all cops drank coffee."

"I'm on duty this afternoon until midnight. I'll be drinking my daily quota of caffeine then."

Ridge winced. "Rough hours."

"Comes with the job." She set her menu down. "You were telling me about the ranch and your rodeo career."

He sat back, relaxing into the conversation. Normally, Ridge avoided talking about himself and his family, but opening up to Elena was easy. As he talked, the hum of twirling overhead fans and loud chatter faded into the background.

"Growing up the son of an alcoholic isn't easy. One day, Dad was great. Loving. Attentive. Teaching me how to rope or helping me build model cars. The next day, he'd be hungover and in bed until noon. Or he'd disappear for days. When he was killed, let's just say kids can be cruel. Whatever remarks their parents made about my dad at home, the kids used them to taunt me at school. My dad was a drunk. A loser. A lazy bum. I struggled and became what the school counselor called moody and withdrawn. I might have gotten into a fight or two." He tried to make light of his troubled youth.

Elena's expression softened. "I'm sorry, Ridge."

"Mom thrived on being angry. At Dad, at God, at life in general. No one was safe. She vented her wrath on anyone and everyone. Gracie left before the ink was dry on her high school diploma. She came back a few years later after bumping around the southwest and 'finding herself.'" He emphasized the last two words and then chuckled. "I shouldn't criticize. She had her ways of coping, and I had mine."

"Is that when she met Jake?" Elena asked. "After she returned?"

"Yep. He joined the sheriff's department while she was away. They met her third day home and fell head over heels in love. Married less than a year later."

"That's sweet."

Ridge nodded. "They balance each other."

"You say that like you're surprised."

"Our parents weren't exactly the best role models for a good marriage. I've often wondered, when the time came, if Gracie and I would have the tools we needed to make a long-term relationship successful. She clearly figured it out. I'm less sure about myself."

The reality was, Ridge had yet to be in a relationship that lasted more than a year. To be fair, much of that was because of his rodeo career. Constant travel took its toll on a couple. But he wondered if the real reason was that, unlike his sister, he hadn't figured out what tools he'd need.

"Awareness is half the battle," Elena said. "And the right person is the other half. That's what I learned from my parents."

He smiled. "Good philosophy."

"Did you also leave after high school?" she asked, changing the subject.

"My uncle introduced me to rodeoing when I was about fifteen. His way of trying to drag me out of my shell."

She smiled. "It seems to have succeeded. You don't strike me as moody and withdrawn."

"You haven't seen me on a bad day."

Their server chose that moment to reappear with a mug of hot water and a basket of various herbal teas. Ridge was thankful for the interruption. Otherwise, Elena might have noticed his utter captivation with her.

"You ready to order?" the young man asked.

She nodded. "I'll have the avocado toast."

Ridge chose biscuits and gravy with two fried eggs on the side and a large orange juice.

Elena gawked at him. "I'm gaining two pounds just looking at all those carbs."

"Renovating the ranch is good for burning calories. So was rodeoing, not to mention good for someone with issues and needing an outlet to vent them." He sipped his coffee. "I did well and saved the bulk of my winnings. I always planned to renovate the ranch. It sat mostly empty for the last ten years, which makes my job harder. No one was there to keep the place up."

"You didn't come home?"

"Not often. Every few months for a few days to visit Gracie and Jake and the girls."

"What about your mom?" Elena asked. "Where's she now?"

"She moved to Sierra Vista once I began rodeoing professionally. Dad left the ranch to me and Gracie. Another reason for her to be angry at him. She refused to stay there after that."

"Ouch. She got nothing from his estate?"

"Life insurance. It was enough for her to make a fresh start in Bisbee where things turned out for the best. She has a good job and married a nice guy who treats her well. I keep hoping her happiness with him will rub off on her and that we might get along better."

"Is that possible?"

"Who knows? She thinks Gracie and I should sell the ranch. For the longest time I wasn't sure what I wanted to do with my life after quitting rodeo. Then something changed. Turning thirty maybe? I was always convinced nothing remained for me in Ironwood Creek. Until I finally realized I was running away from my past rather than facing it. Does that make sense?"

"It does. I've felt the same way myself at times. It's one of the reasons I decided to transfer to a new town."

They had something in common. He liked that.

"My plan is to buy Gracie out at some point, if she's agreeable," Ridge said. "She's not attached to the place like I am."

"You seem to enjoy fixing it up."

"Renovating the ranch is my dream. More than that, I'm convinced it's God's plan for me. Does that sound crazy?"

"Not at all. I believe law enforcement is God's plan for me."

Another thing in common. This was getting better and better.

"No more rodeoing, then?" she asked.

"Naw." Ridge shook his head. "I'm tired of life on the road and the aches and pains. I want to make a fresh start here. We still had a few head of cattle when I was little. My dad sold them off, along with most everything else. If something could be converted into drinking money, it was. Once I finish repairing the fences, think I'll invest in a new herd. Raise cattle like my grandfather."

"That's great, Ridge. Your plans, I mean. For the ranch and making your home in Ironwood Creek."

"What about you? Are you contemplating putting down roots in our little town?"

"I think so. Yeah." She glanced out the café's large picture window with its view of the street's quaint mixture of old and modern western ambience. "I like it here."

"Our first female deputy." Ridge didn't hide his admiration. "That has to come with some challenges. Ironwood Creek isn't as progressive as places like Phoenix and Tucson."

She laughed. "A few challenges, yes. Fortunately, I have some experience working with male law enforcement officers. My dad's a detective for the Phoenix Police Department. My grandfather's a retired sergeant with the Buckeye PD."

"Really? Third generation. I'm impressed, Deputy Tomes."

"I think my dad was counting on my brother carrying the torch. Instead, I am. My brother wants to be a graphic artist."

"Interesting." Ridge studied her. "So, why Ironwood Creek and not something closer to your family?"

"Several reasons. My dad and grandfather are well-known in Phoenix area law enforcement circles. I wanted to go someplace where they were less known and feel confident any promotions or special accommodations I received were because I'd earned them and not because of my last name."

"Makes sense."

"When the opening came up in Ironwood Creek, I liked the idea of a small town, and I thought my efforts might stand out more in a field of fewer deputies."

Their food arrived then, and they both dug in. After a few

moments, Ridge got to the point. "So tell me, what did you want to talk about?"

"I researched the town's history like you suggested, and you were right. It's unsavory. And unsettling that it went on for years and years unchecked."

"There's a reason for that. Money. It buys silence and co-operation."

"True." She took another bite. "I also researched your dad. There wasn't much to find. Nothing you don't already know, I'm sure." She filled him in. Ridge ate in silence, listening. "I was going to forget the whole thing," she continued, "until Jake warned me to stay out of it."

Ridge's head shot up. "Warned you how?"

"He doesn't want you winding up in danger like your dad. And he said I would, too, if I wasn't careful."

"That sounds almost threatening."

"It wasn't. If he came across strong, it's because he cares."

Even so, Ridge worried for her safety. "The last thing I want is for anything to happen to you."

"Nothing will." She set down her knife and fork, seeming to struggle for words.

"What is it?"

Elena firmed her jaw. "I'd like to help you find out who killed your dad."

Ridge stared at her, taken aback. "I'm sure I must have heard wrong. I thought you said you wanted to help me."

Their server abruptly appeared. "Can I get you anything else?"

And then, Elena's phone rang, bringing their conversation to a grinding halt.

While Ridge ordered more coffee for him and tea for Elena, she talked to her mom. Her attempts to cut the conversation short and return the phone call later were thwarted. Her highly observant mom had instantly jumped to a wrong conclusion and insisted Elena reveal the name of her deep-voiced companion.

"You're on a date?"

"We're having lunch, Mom."

"Lunch or *lunch*?"

Elena bit her tongue rather than rise to the bait her mom dangled. "It's not like that. We're working on a case together."

"I want to hear everything. What case? Where did you meet him? Is he good-looking?"

She sighed. "I'll call you in an hour, Mom."

"You'd better, *mija*."

Thankfully pocketing her phone, she refocused on Ridge. Same as he was focusing on her. She enjoyed the moment for a few heartbeats. No harm in that, was there? Her next thought was of her mom's unending questions.

"Sorry. My mom doesn't always take the hint."

"You two are close," Ridge said. "That's nice."

"It is. Most of the time. When she doesn't have her nose in my business."

"She cares, Elena." There was a trace of wistfulness in his voice. "You're blessed."

Though curious about his relationship with his mom, she sidestepped the personal and potentially sensitive subject. "I meant what I said about helping you, Ridge."

"I'm glad. Seriously. But I have to ask why."

"I talked to the chief the other day. Asked him what he knew of your dad's murder and the drug trafficking. It clearly struck a nerve. He shut me down and suggested I mind my own business."

"You don't appear to be doing that."

"My interest was piqued. I had to ask myself, what wasn't he telling me?"

Ridge considered briefly. "The chief has always seemed to me to be a decent man. He probably shut you down because he's worried about you, like Jake is, and believes the cartel is still around. Just lying low."

"That's not it." Elena dunked a tea bag in her fresh cup of hot water. "He's hiding something."

Ridge sat forward. "Like what?"

"I don't know. He's been at the station a long time. Oscar Wentworth, too. The chief was promoted from sergeant deputy when the former chief retired. There's a picture of him and the former chief hanging on the wall in the station."

"I remember my mom talking about Dempsey's promotion. There was apparently some bad blood between him and Wentworth at the time because they both wanted the job. And then between Wentworth and Jake when Jake was promoted to sergeant deputy."

"I can see that," Elena mused aloud, thinking of her co-worker and his short fuse. "You don't suppose there's a connection between the chief's promotion and your dad's homicide?"

"What kind of connection?"

She sighed. "Forget it. I'm grasping at straws. The chief wasn't promoted until years after your dad's homicide." She sipped her tea, knowing she should ignore the direction her thoughts had taken, but not quite able to do that. "You said there were people who stood to benefit from the drug trafficking. What people were you referring to?"

"Higher-ups. Elected officials. The former chief. The mayor. Council members. Property owners who took kickbacks to look the other way, one of whom may or may not have been my dad."

"Him taking kickbacks would make sense, I hate to say. Money is all too often a motive for murder."

Ridge studied her. "You think Chief Dempsey is protecting certain people? Or himself?"

"No." Elena heard the lack of conviction in her voice. "But I keep asking myself why the drug trafficking went on for so long before anyone put a stop to it. And three homicides were swept under the carpet. All of them unsolved. Did you know that?"

"I did." Ridge sat back, a slight smile tugging at the corners of his mouth. "Seems like we have our work cut out for us, partner."

"I'm wondering how much help I can be with both Jake and the chief keeping a watch on me."

"They have a point, Elena. There could be risks. And you have no vested interest in my dad's case. Unless…" He paused.

"What?"

"Don't take this wrong, but are you trying to prove yourself to the chief?"

"It's not that," she insisted. *Not only that.*

"Then what?"

How could she explain? "I have this thing about putting right what's wrong and seeing the bad guys brought to justice."

"Ah. You're a do-gooder."

"If I am, that's fine with me."

Elena had lost her grandmother under terrible circumstances. Her death had affected Elena profoundly and was responsible, in part, for shaping her into the person she was today—someone determined to make the world a better place. She didn't talk about the tragedy with just anyone, not until she felt confident and comfortable in the relationship.

"It's more than fine," Ridge said.

She sat up straighter. "Your dad didn't deserve to be killed. Finding his murderer would vindicate him and see that justice is served. But I'll admit that yes, if it shows the chief and the others that I'm good at my job and deserving of their respect, that would be an added bonus."

Ridge reached across the table for her hand. "Elena. You're the first one to believe me. And the first one to offer help. That means a lot."

She quite liked the sensation his fingers enveloping hers evoked. So much for ignoring her response to him.

"I'm not the first person. People believed you, Ridge. That was the trouble. They discredited you to protect themselves."

"Thank you." He grinned in earnest. "Where do we start?"

"Start what?" came an unexpected voice.

They both looked up. Elena gave a small jerk.

Jake stood at their table. Beside him, Gracie stared, her eyes riveted on Elena and Ridge's clasped hands.

"Isn't this nice," she said. "We have the table next to yours."

Elena quickly reclaimed her hand, which only drew further attention to her and Ridge. Her cheeks heated with embarrassment.

Ridge acted as if nothing was out of the ordinary. Standing, he asked amiably, "What brings you here?"

"Lunch." Jake hadn't taken his eyes off Elena. "Same as you."

Their young server motioned. "Would you like me to push the tables together?"

"We're nearly finished," Ridge said.

At the same time, Gracie nudged her daughters forward and overruled him by proclaiming, "Perfect! Thank you."

Tables quickly joined, the server took the newcomers' drink orders. Moments later, Elena found herself sitting next to Gracie. Jake continued to stare at her from his seat next to Ridge. He looked like he might have guessed why they were here and wasn't happy about it.

Well, so be it. She and Ridge weren't doing anything wrong.

"You remember our girls, Lindsey and Laney?" Gracie asked. "Say hello, girls."

"Hello," the pair answered in unison before returning their attention to the video playing on their dad's phone.

"What are you two really doing here?" Jake asked, disapproval darkening his features.

"Biscuits and gravy." Ridge pointed to his almost empty plate with his fork.

"Why?" Jake addressed the question to Elena.

She deflected. "We were hungry."

"I don't buy it," he scoffed.

"Jake. Enough." Gracie sent Elena an apologetic smile.

"If you must know," Ridge said, "we were talking about movies and trying to pick one we both like."

"You're going to the movies?" Gracie pressed a hand to her heart. "Like a date?"

"We were discussing it."

Elena gaped at Ridge. He, in turn, sent her a reassuring head nod. She had to either trust him or cause a minor scene.

Their server returned with drinks. He refilled Ridge's coffee, then took food orders for the rest of them before disappearing.

"Be honest, Elena. What's it like working with my husband?" Gracie asked with pronounced glee.

Elena swallowed, telling herself she could get through this. "He's very good at his job. Thorough. Knowledgeable. I've learned a lot from him."

The remainder of their meal was an exercise in patience and endurance. Gracie's unabashed curiosity and Jake's relentless scrutiny knew no bounds. At last, she and Ridge were able to make their excuses—she was on duty in a few hours. He settled the tab, refusing to let her pay half or cover the tip.

"Bye. See you soon," Gracie trilled after them.

"Where's your car?" Ridge asked once they were outside.

"Over there." Elena indicated a compact hybrid, and they started walking. "Your family thinks we're dating now."

He chuckled. "Is that so terrible?"

"Yes. Because we're not."

"You have to admit, it's a great cover. No one will question us when we're together working on my dad's case."

She couldn't dispute that logic. At her car, she fished her phone from her purse and said, "We should exchange numbers."

"Good idea."

He gave her his, and she sent him a quick text.

"I'm thinking we should talk to the detective on your dad's case, assuming he's still around," she added. "I'll find out what I can and call you tomorrow."

"And I'll keep looking for the gold chain. It may have been buried with the gun and money, and I missed it."

"Okay."

"Thanks again, Elena."

She started to answer him when her phone pinged with a notification. Without thinking, she checked the display. The text was from a number she didn't recognize. The first few words were visible and jumped off the screen at her, striking like small daggers. Her finger automatically swiped to open the message.

"Elena, are you okay?"

Her face must have gone white for Ridge grabbed her by the arm to steady her.

She held out the phone to him, her blood running cold. "Read this."

Quit looking into Burnham's death or you'll end up dead like him.

FOUR

"You must be scared, Deputy. I want you to take a few days off."

"I'm not scared, Chief, I'm mad."

Elena sat across from her boss in his office. She'd reported the threatening text immediately after receiving it. Ridge, who'd been more upset than her, refused to let her out of his sight. He'd followed her home from the café and then insisted on accompanying her while she inspected every square inch of her apartment. She'd refused him, citing law enforcement policy, only to grudgingly let him in when her initial sweep revealed no evidence of an intruder or a break-in.

Reminding him that, between the two of them, she was the one trained for this type of situation had no effect. He'd remained adamant and conducted his own inspection.

When he'd finished, she called the unfamiliar number. No surprise, a message played after the first ring telling Elena she'd reached a number that had been disconnected or was no longer in service.

A burner phone, probably. She'd heard about ways to fake automated recordings.

Ridge left only when she promised to call him in an hour and again when she reached the station. She'd half-suspected that he'd remain in the parking lot, surveying her unit. She understood. He felt responsible for her receiving the threatening text even though she'd volunteered to help him.

Of course, he'd insisted they drop the investigation into his dad's case, and Elena told him they'd talk about it later. She wasn't easily intimidated.

The chief had called her into his office the second she arrived at work. They'd been chatting for the past twenty minutes.

"I don't like being threatened," Elena continued.

"You like being foolish?" he retorted. His chair squeaked when he rocked back. "Someone figured out what you're up to, and they're not joking around."

"Who?" she demanded. "And how?"

"There's a record of every keystroke you type on that computer."

"Are you accusing somebody within the sheriff's department of threatening me?"

"I'm saying you and your actions are visible. A lot of people saw you with Ridge earlier at the café."

And church, she silently added. Ironwood Creek wasn't so large that the news of a gun and money discovered on the Burnham Ranch hadn't spread like a gasoline fire. If someone had something to hide—say, for instance, that they were involved with Pete Burnham's death—they might conclude Ridge and Elena were trading information. Especially if they spotted the pair with their heads bent together in a serious conversation.

"What are you going to do about the text, Chief?"

"For starters, you're on desk duty for the time being."

"Chief!"

"Oscar's on his way in."

She groaned. "You wouldn't restrict me if I was a man."

The chief's expression darkened. "Your gender has nothing to do with this."

She didn't believe him. "What, then? I get to type reports and answer the phone?"

"Let's see what happens over the next day or two. You contact admin?"

"On the drive here." The sheriff's department took threats against their personnel very seriously.

"What did they say?"

"I filed a report. There's not much they can do under the circumstances. The threat is vague, and I haven't been attacked or approached. I called my phone company, but they won't tell me anything useful without a warrant."

"Speaking of a warrant, have you called the police? Because I think you should. In fact, I'm telling you to call them."

"I will." And she would. If only to create a record, should there be another threat. Sheriff's departments and local police had different jurisdictions, but they worked together to keep the peace and solve crimes. Besides, the person who threatened Elena may not be from Ironwood Creek. "They won't do much, either. Not unless something more happens."

Elena remembered Jake finding her and Ridge in the café and questioning them. Would he have sent the text? Not that she believed for an instant he'd hurt her, but he had warned her to steer clear of Ridge. This could be his attempt to scare her away.

An idea occurred to her. "You know, Chief, the text could be proof."

"Of what?"

"A connection between Pete Burnham's death and the drug trafficking. Whoever's involved is getting nervous."

"The person could also be a quack. Or pulling a prank."

"Some prank."

"People get their kicks out of toying with law enforcement, or they have an axe to grind."

"You really believe that?" she said.

"I'm not discounting anything."

"The gun and money most likely belonged to one of the drug runners. Maybe the guy Ridge saw arguing with his dad."

"We'll learn more when the lab forwards the test results."

Elena nodded. When she'd asked, Sage confirmed that the packages arrived on Friday. She'd also let Elena know that the chief had indeed requested a rush. That was unexpected, given how indifferent he'd seemed at first. Sage had gone on to tell Elena that rush requests seldom guaranteed quick results, which came when they came.

"What if Pete Burnham happened upon the drug runner burying the gun and money and was killed for it?" Elena asked the chief.

"That's doubtful." He opened his desk drawer, removed a bottle of antacid tablets and popped three in his mouth. "First of all, why would the drug runner have buried the gun and money on private property? Second, he wouldn't have bothered to take Burnham into the hills behind the ranch. He'd have offed him right there and left the body."

Elena had thought the same thing, but asked anyway. "Like the other two murders?"

"Exactly. Those men were shot right outside their backdoors. Burnham, on the other hand, was pushed off a ledge into a ravine."

"But they were locals like Pete Burnham. And the drug runners were using their land."

"Allegedly," the chief hedged.

"There were witnesses."

"There were people who reported seeing nighttime activity on the victims' properties prior to the murders. Not specifically on the nights of the murders," he emphasized. "No weapons were found. No evidence. Not a single lead uncovered in any of the cases."

"Until now," Elena said.

"Maybe." The chief returned the bottle of antacids to his desk drawer. "Assuming DNA evidence can be lifted from the gun and the money, and assuming it can be connected to someone in the system. Both are highly unlikely."

He was right. She and Ridge would just have to search elsewhere. And be discreet. One good thing about desk duty, she'd have time for research…except if the chief's earlier suggestion was correct, someone might be tracking her computer usage. She'd have to find another way.

The door to the station opened, and the chief craned his neck to see past her.

Oscar called out, "Hi, honey, I'm home."

Elena resisted rolling her eyes. The other deputy, twenty-seven years her senior, was biding his time until he could retire. Like her, he'd transferred from another part of the state and now called Ironwood Creek his home. He made no secret of wanting to return to the Flagstaff area one day.

"We'll be done here in a minute," the chief said.

They heard him cross to the breakroom, where he'd stow his personal belongings and prepare to go out on patrol. *Him* instead of Elena. The thought left an unpleasant taste in her mouth. Desk duty felt like a punishment rather than the chief protecting her from danger.

"You going to be all right if I head home?" the chief asked. "My son and his family are coming for dinner."

"I'll be fine, sir."

"Call if there's a problem or you get another threat—or even if you're afraid. You don't have to act tough, Elena. You have nothing to prove to us."

His remark gave her pause. That was the only time he'd ever come close to acknowledging she received different treatment than the men. For a moment, and only a moment, Elena's hard shell softened.

"I will. Call, that is."

"Okay. Good." The chief stood and reached for his jacket laying on the credenza behind him. "I'll see you tomorrow."

She followed him out of his office and into the main room.

Oscar sat at Elena's preferred desk, stroking his prominent mustache as he read. She swallowed down her annoyance and sat across from him. He'd chosen her desk solely to irritate her, and she wouldn't give him the satisfaction of seeing that his ploy worked.

After the chief left, she occupied herself with grunt work, pretending to be too busy to chat with Oscar. Sunday evenings were notoriously slow in Ironwood Creek. Just when Elena thought she might have to suffer Oscar's boorish company for hours on end, a call came in about a disturbance at Liberty Market, and he escaped. A relief, no doubt, to them both.

Rather than get on the computer, Elena went to the storeroom. She didn't hold much hope of finding anything interesting, since most of the sheriff's department's records were digitized. But there were some older paper records she'd noticed on previous research deep dives. It was worth a try.

While she was rifling through files, she called Ridge on her cell phone. He answered immediately.

"How are you doing?"

"I've been grounded. The chief put me on desk duty."

"Good."

Were all men alike? "I didn't call to talk about that," she said a little grumpily. "Are you near a computer?"

"I have a laptop."

"Can you do a basic search on the Bisbee detective assigned to your dad's homicide? His name was Frank Darnelly."

"I remember him. A tall guy. Imposing. Never cracked a smile."

Which would have intimidated a twelve-year-old.

"I don't want to use the station's computer," she explained, "in case someone is monitoring my usage."

"Is that possible?"

"It is for anyone with access to Cochise County's network." She pulled a new box from the shelf. "I'm just being extra cautious. Half the town knows I was the responding deputy to your ranch and that we went to lunch after church."

"That's true. Hang on a second."

She heard muffled noises in the background.

"Got my laptop open."

"Start by conducting a basic search with his name and a few other key words like Bisbee and police detective. Don't be surprised if you find nothing. People in law enforcement try not to be easily found."

"I think this is him," Ridge said a minute later and read off the limited details. "How many Francis Darnellys could there be living in Bisbee?"

"Let's hope only one."

"There's no address or phone number. We could pay twenty-nine dollars for a background report."

"I have a better idea. My cousin's wife works for motor vehicles. She can probably get me Darnelly's address. He's retired now."

"Then what? Drive to Bisbee and knock on his door?"

"Actually, yes."

"When's your next day off?"

She replaced the lid on the box of useless files and pushed to her feet. There was nothing of value in the storeroom. "Tuesday."

"I'll pick you up after lunch. One o'clock?"

"Let's make it four-thirty. Bisbee is thirty miles away. He's more likely to be home at dinnertime. I'll meet you at Valley View Bank." The station phone rang then. "Gotta run."

She disconnected before he could say more.

Ridge sat on a plush visitor chair in the Valley View Bank lobby. Elena was supposed to have been here by now. In hindsight, they probably should have met at her apartment. But Elena had wanted to be careful should anyone be following them. Too late now.

Twice, he'd had to fend off a cheerful clerk who wanted to know if he could be of assistance. His mistake. He should have probably waited in his truck. Except someone just sitting in a truck tended to draw the wrong kind of attention. But so did a six-foot cowboy sitting in a bank lobby. Maybe he should ask about opening an account.

Fidgeting, he checked his phone again. Had something happened to Elena? Another threat? She'd sent a vague two-word text that hadn't relieved him.

Running late.

He was about to call her when the bank's glass doors swooshed open, and she entered, red-faced from either exertion or the freezing wind, a leftover from yesterday's nasty weather front. At least they wouldn't have to battle rain on their drive to Bisbee. The wind, for all its cold, had dispatched the clouds.

Ridge shoved out of the visitor chair and strode across the small lobby toward her. Customers, hurrying to complete their transactions before the bank closed stared briefly and then glanced away.

"Sorry I'm late," she said. "There was an accident on Ocotillo Street. Traffic had to detour. No one appeared badly hurt."

Ridge caught her by the elbow and escorted her back outside. "Let's leave before we draw too much attention."

"We should take my car," Elena said. "It's less recognizable in town than your truck with its custom license plate."

"Nah, I'll drive. If our cover is that we're on a date, it will appear less suspicious should someone spot us and we're in my truck." He didn't acknowledge her weary, sometimes-women-drive-on-dates expression. "There's a restaurant in Bisbee, Rusty's Steakhouse. I checked, and it's not far from where Frank Darnelly lives. We can say we had dinner there if anyone asks."

"I'm impressed." She smiled. "You're better at this covert stuff than I'd expected."

He opened the passenger-side door of his truck, and she hopped in. During the drive, they shared what they'd each accomplished during the last two days.

"I've turned the ranch upside-down trying to find the gold chain," Ridge said as they headed out of town. "Mom tossed or donated most of Dad's things after he died. She didn't want any reminders of him. I scoured every closet and drawer and cabinet in the house. Looked under mattresses. Flipped through the pages of books. Went through old boxes. I even called my mom and my uncle. Neither of them recalled anything about a gold chain."

"Other than potential DNA evidence and validating your story," Elena said, "I'm not sure what else locating it would prove."

"If we showed the chain around town, someone may recognize it and be able to identify the guy my dad argued with."

"That's a stretch, but it's not impossible," Elena conceded. "Still, I think we'll have better results focusing elsewhere. Like talking to Frank Darnelly and researching records. I went to the public library yesterday hoping to find some information on the other two unsolved homicides."

Ridge merged onto the highway leading to Bisbee. "Learn anything?"

"The only connection I found between the other homicides and your dad's was all three men owned land that sat between town and the mountains—land that accessed the landing strip."

"What landing strip?" Ridge asked.

"There's a long stretch of flat ground hidden behind Rooster Butte. I read about it in one of the reports. Small planes would meet the cartel's vehicles there and transfer their product. The planes then flew off to Phoenix or Vegas or whatever large city was their destination. The empty trucks returned to the border for another load."

"How did I not know this?"

"You were young," Elena told him. "Why would you know?"

Ridge decided to call his mom again tomorrow and ask her about the landing strip and their ranch's proximity to it.

"I spoke to the librarian," Elena continued. "She's lived in Ironwood Creek for over twenty years. She told me the drug trafficking and the landing strip were an open secret in town. Everyone knew, but no one talked about it."

"Because they were afraid," Ridge said.

"Or they benefited."

He thought once more of his parents. What was his mom not telling him?

The GPS voice on his phone advised him to take the next exit.

"How do you think the detective will react when we show up at his door?" He turned right at the stoplight.

"He won't talk at first." Elena shook her head. "Not without a lot of convincing."

"Do you have a plan?"

"I think you should take the lead. Appeal to him as a murdered man's son who's seeking closure. He'll act tough and indifferent, but he'll have a heart somewhere in there."

"Won't he respond better to you as a fellow law enforcement officer?"

"No." She glanced out the window. "He's old-school."

Ridge studied her profile. For a small woman, she was a warrior with the courage of David and the wisdom of Daniel. She knew when to fight and when to remain quiet and let others take up the sword.

Before long, they were passing rows of buildings and houses exhibiting Bisbee's iconic and eclectic architecture. Examples of the town's colorful mining history were evident everywhere. Shops and art galleries and coffee shops abounded. Tourists walked shoulder to shoulder on the sidewalks.

Ridge navigated the busy street, switching from one lane

to the other in an attempt to avoid delays and reach Darnelly's house before dinnertime.

More than once, he noticed a gray sedan in his rear-or side-view mirror. He asked Elena about it. She kept an eye on the car, which turned left two intersections later and didn't appear again.

Frank Darnelly lived in an attractive middle-class neighborhood. Ridge had found out that the retired detective was married and a proud grandfather, thanks to his wife who was very active on social media.

He parked on the street in front of the house rather than pull into the driveway. "Ready?" he asked Elena. She'd been quiet since her remark about Darnelly being old-school. Ridge didn't presume to understand what she went through, a young woman trying to make her way in a male-dominated profession.

She smiled at him. "Here we go."

At the front door, Ridge rang the video doorbell. He mentally rehearsed what he'd say if Darnelly answered or if his wife did. As it turned out, they were greeted by a disembodied voice from a tiny speaker.

"What do you want?"

Ridge swallowed, composing himself. Not what he'd been expecting. "Detective Darnelly?"

"Who wants to know?"

"My name is Ridge Burnham. I'm Pete Burnham's son. You were the detective assigned to his homicide investigation eighteen years ago."

A long silence followed. Finally, Darnelly repeated, "What do you want?"

"I found some potential evidence buried on my family's ranch. It may be connected to my dad's homicide. I was hoping you'd be willing to talk to me. To us."

"Who's your friend?"

Elena removed her badge from her jacket pocket and held it up to the smart doorbell's camera. "Deputy Elena Tomes with the Cochise County Sheriff's Department. I'm currently stationed at Ironwood Creek."

"Are you here in an official capacity?"

"No, sir. I'm the deputy who responded to Mr. Burnham's call when he discovered the potential evidence, but I'm here strictly as a friend."

Her answer was followed by another long silence.

"Detective Darnelly," Ridge said, deciding to appeal to the man's heart as Elena had suggested, "I've spent almost two decades living with uncertainty and anger and frustration. Struggling to put my past behind me. If there's anything you could tell us that might help find the person who killed my dad, or at least help me learn why he was killed, I'd appreciate it. As would my sister, Gracie. You may remember her."

More silence. Ridge exchanged a glance with Elena. He was about to give up and walk away when the door opened and a tall, lanky bald man stood glowering at them.

He retreated a step and motioned to them. "Come in. Wipe your feet first."

They did, and he ushered Ridge and Elena inside. His wife either wasn't home or had been instructed to stay out of sight.

"We're sorry to disturb you," Ridge started.

When he went to remove his jacket, Darnelly's brows drew together in a way that implied Ridge and Elena wouldn't be staying long enough to make themselves comfortable. He didn't offer them a seat. Instead, they stood awkwardly in the foyer.

"What did you discover on your property?" Darnelly asked.

"A handgun—a .40 caliber revolver. And a strongbox containing forty thousand dollars. They were buried beneath my well house. From the looks of them, they were there a long time."

"Is the money counterfeit?"

Ridge drew back. He hadn't considered that possibility.

Evidently, Elena had for she said, "On inspection, the money appeared to be legit. The lab in Tucson will confirm."

The older man considered. "I doubt they'll find much trace evidence if the gun and money are eighteen years old. There's a lot of moisture under a well house."

Ridge refused to be deterred. "Is there anything you can tell us that wasn't in the report and could shed light on my dad's case?"

Again, Darnelly paused before answering. "For what it's worth, I always believed you about the stranger you saw arguing with your dad earlier in the day. I did investigate. Interviewed the neighbors and people in town. No one saw a bearded man with long shaggy hair that day or any day before or after. I checked arrests for the next year. Anyone remotely resembling the man you described had an alibi on the day of Pete Burnham's murder."

Ridge felt a rush coursing through him. Someone had believed him and made an effort to find his dad's murderer. He'd had no idea. "Thank you for telling me, Detective."

The hard edges of Darnelly's expression smoothed. "I'm sorry you lost your dad. That had to be rough. But there's nothing I can tell you that will help. Do I think the gun and money you found were buried by the man who shoved him over that ledge? Maybe. Likely not. I'd say your dad buried it, and if any DNA evidence comes back, it'll be his."

"Where do *you* think he got the money?"

"Where everyone in Ironwood Creek acquired large sums of cash in those days."

"The drug cartel?"

Darnelly shrugged.

Ridge wanted to believe his dad was innocent of any wrongdoing, but facts were beginning to pile up and point to the opposite. His dad had been arguing with a stranger who threatened him and his family. He'd gone back on an agreement. Even if Ridge could discover who'd murdered his dad, he wouldn't be able to vindicate him.

"My guess is your dad was receiving a kickback from the cartel," Darnelly said. "Or he stole the money."

"My dad was honest."

"Your dad had a drinking problem. He nearly ran that ranch of yours into the ground. Folks in a position like his don't always exercise good judgment. If the cartel came to him with a deal, he probably took it."

"He may have been trying, in his way, to provide for his family," Elena offered.

Ridge recognized her attempt to justify his dad's actions and fresh grief weighed on him. Less for his dad and more for the loss of a belief he'd held most of his life.

He caught Elena's concerned expression and tried to silently assure her that he was all right. Only he was far from all right. His world had shifted, and nothing would be quite the same after today.

The retired detective blew out a long, weary breath. "The cartel wielded a significant amount of influence and power back in those days. They still do. You need to be careful. Ask too many questions, and news will reach the wrong set of ears sooner or later."

"Whose ears?" Elena asked.

"You need to leave." Darnelly hitched his chin at the door.

Before Ridge could say more, Elena tugged on his arm. "Thank you, Detective."

Standing on the threshold, Darnelly issued them a final warning. "Take my advice. Let sleeping dogs lie. You might want closure or answers, but it's not worth risking your life. Or anyone else's." His glance cut to Elena before returning to Ridge. "Chances are good your dad got mixed up with the wrong people. Don't you make the same mistake."

With that, he shut the door in their faces.

FIVE

Ridge and Elena returned to his truck and drove the first mile in silence. He didn't want to admit how shaken the encounter with the retired detective had left him.

Avoiding Elena's concerned expression, he asked, "Do you think Darnelly was serious about the cartel still being active in Ironwood Creek?"

"He definitely believes it. Whether he's right or wrong, I can't tell you. I haven't seen any indication of their presence, but I haven't been a resident very long."

"And up until six months ago, I was gone a lot."

"They could be operating on the lowdown," she admitted. "Technology is constantly evolving. Makes it easy to carry out a sophisticated illegal operation under everyone's noses."

"In Ironwood Creek? How?"

"Drones. Hidden cameras and listening devices. Computer hacking. Spies."

"Spies?" Ridge scoffed.

"It's not that far-fetched. The cartel is a powerful and wealthy organization. Though it's more likely, in my opinion, they moved away from Ironwood Creek and went somewhere else." She scrolled through her phone. "I'll see what I can find out."

"Be careful, Elena."

"I will."

They crawled through the center of Bisbee, keeping pace

with the other slow-moving vehicles. Evening had fallen while they were with Darnelly, coming early this time of year. Storefronts and office building windows glowed bright against an increasingly darkening sky.

"Are you hungry?" Ridge asked.

"A little."

"We can stop. What are you in the mood for?"

"I hate to ask, considering your regular diet of fast food, but can we get drive-through? I have an early morning dentist appointment before my shift starts and need to get home."

"Hamburgers or tacos?"

"Hamburgers." She pointed ahead. "What about that place we saw on the way into town?"

Ridge changed lanes. When he did, he noticed a pair of headlights changing lanes with him. He thought nothing of it until they stopped at the next light. Observing the car in his side mirror, he noticed the shape of it looked remarkably like the gray sedan that had stuck close to them during their earlier trip through town. Then again, the make and model were hardly unique.

He abruptly changed lanes and turned right at the next intersection.

"What are you doing?" Elena asked.

Ridge waited to answer until the sedan also turned. "I think we have a tail."

"Are you sure?" She cranked her head around.

"Don't look. You'll just draw attention to us."

Going faster wasn't possible, not with the congested traffic. Ridge did his best to outmaneuver the car, to no avail. It stayed with them, occasionally dropping back but always catching up again.

Elena opened the search app on her phone and began typing. "We could drive to the police station four blocks away. That'll lose them."

Without signaling, Ridge pulled into a fried chicken place. The car went past and continued up the road.

"Is he gone?"

"For now."

"Do we wait?" Elena asked.

"We might as well get something to eat."

She gaped at him. "You can eat after that? What if he comes back?"

"If someone was tailing us, they know we came here to see Darnelly and that we're heading home to Ironwood Creek. Us eating won't change anything. Besides, if they were going to shoot us, they'd have done so by now. Probably when we were leaving Darnelly's."

To Ridge's surprise, and, okay, his enjoyment, Elena chuckled. "Okay. Let's have some chicken."

"You're not scared?"

"I'm more cautious than scared. You're right, if their intent was to kill us, we'd be dead by now. In my opinion, they were gathering intel."

"I agree."

"They may have been watching Darnelly more than us. Or just making sure he didn't talk."

Ridge studied her. "You think he's covering up something?"

"He could be protecting someone. One of those higher-ups you mentioned."

"You may be onto something."

They opted to go inside the restaurant rather than hit the drive-through. Fried chicken wasn't the easiest food to consume while driving.

"Should we sit by the window?" Ridge pointed to a table after they got their orders. "That way, we can keep an eye out for the car.

"He realized we made him and that his intimidation tactics didn't work. He may not come back."

"Or if he does, he could be driving a different vehicle."

"Let's sit where we can see out the window, but aren't an easy target." Elena chose a table in the center of the small dining area. "We should also watch for a tail when we leave."

They dug into their meals. Adrenaline surges from being followed apparently worked up an appetite.

"Did you tell anyone where we were going today?" Ridge asked between bites.

"The chief and Sage, the station secretary. It's my day off, but I'm potentially on call if needed. I didn't mention what we planned or that we were seeing Darnelly, only that I'd be in Bisbee. What about you?"

"I didn't say a word."

"Even to Jake?" she probed.

"Especially not to him. Or my sister. I went so far as to sign out of the family tracking app we all have on our phones for emergencies."

"Will Gracie notice and question you?"

"Since she has no idea I left town, and I answered her when she texted me a while ago, no. At least, I don't think she will."

"Well, somebody figured out our plans."

"The same person who sent you that text?"

"Maybe."

"That leaves the chief and the secretary."

Elena furrowed her brow. "Actually, Sage keeps everyone's whereabouts on a daily log in case she's at lunch or something and one of us needs the information."

"Who has access to the daily log?" Ridge asked.

"It's right there on her desk for anyone to see."

He considered this information. "I'm worried about you, Elena."

"I'm more worried about you. You're a bigger threat to the cartel than me. I'm just a means to get to you."

"Still, you could get hurt. Darnelly's warning was no joke."

"I don't intimidate easily, Ridge. If I did, I wouldn't have chosen law enforcement as a profession."

"Maybe you should be intimidated."

"Why don't we put this in God's hands?"

Ridge sat back. "I believe God gives us free will, and I choose to be safe."

"Not what I'm suggesting," Elena said. "Let's take a few days off from investigating. If nothing new develops, if the forensic tests on the gun and money are inconclusive, then perhaps God is giving you your answer. You're not supposed to know what happened to your dad. It won't serve you or the greater good. He wants you to move on."

"And if something does develop?"

"Then we continue investigating."

Ridge deliberated a moment. "All right. Fair enough."

Once they finished eating, they headed home. No one followed them as far as they could tell.

"Are you going to the winter picnic at church on Saturday?" Ridge asked, exiting the highway and taking the road leading into Ironwood Creek. "Gracie's twisting my arm."

"I am, unless I get called in."

"That's four days from now. We can check in with each other there, assuming nothing comes up beforehand."

"Will your sister be expecting us to go together? You did imply we were dating."

Ridge tried to read Elena's expression. How did she feel about their pretend arrangement?

"We could," he said. "Just to keep up appearances for the time being."

"Okay."

She didn't sound enthused. Well, this was business, and not a social outing. He needed to remember that.

"Okay," he echoed. "Pick you up at eleven-thirty? I'll bring the drinks." He strove to lighten the mood. "I make a mean lemonade."

"You have no kitchen."

"I will by then. And I've got to do something with all those lemons."

"That's right, I saw your trees. They're loaded with fruit."

"You're welcome to as many bags as you can carry."

"I may take you up on the offer." She smiled then. "I'm bringing pozole."

"Homemade?"

She feigned offense. "Yes, homemade."

"Elena Tomes. Are you saying you're a good cook?"

"A passable cook. My late grandmother taught me."

Ridge broke into a wide grin. "This I have to try."

Nothing amiss happened for the remainder of the ride home. Ridge pulled into the bank parking lot and drove to where Elena's car sat alone at the rear of the lot, bathed in the yellow glow from a light mounted to the building.

She climbed out of his truck. He did, too, and walked her to her car, relieved nothing awaited her other than a blanket of dried leaves, thanks to the earlier wind.

He couldn't help his sense of alarm when he remembered the text she'd received the other day. She may be well-trained, but she was still small of stature and vulnerable.

"Elena."

Without conscious thought, he drew her into a hug. She resisted at first, then relaxed, her palms resting on the front of his jacket. His arms went around her shoulders in a protective gesture.

"Be careful," he told her.

"I will."

He released her then, taking hold of her hands. "Do you mind if I say a quick prayer?"

"I'd like that."

He bent his head close to hers. "Dear Lord, if we are on the course that You intend for us, we ask that You take us under Your wing and watch over us while we search for answers. Grant us the strength we need to face our adversaries and overcome whatever obstacles lay ahead. We are now and forever Your humble servants. Amen."

"Amen," Elena repeated softly.

Ridge squeezed Elena's fingers. He had no reason to continue keeping her close, but he couldn't bring himself to let her go. Her hands felt right in his as if they belonged there.

All at once, a gray sedan rounded the bank building and came straight at them, headlights on high beam. Elena ripped her hands from Ridge's and spun to confront the intruder, not showing a single trace of fear. Ridge instinctively stepped in front of her, but she'd have none of it and moved out from behind him.

The car came closer and slowed to a stop. With the engine continuing to idle, the door opened.

"It's okay," Elena said, and exhaled in relief. "I know him."

The middle-aged man strode forward. When he entered the light cast by his car's headlights, Ridge also recognized him—though, without the uniform, it took a moment.

"What are you doing here, Oscar?" Elena asked, her tone a mixture of relief and apprehension.

The off-duty deputy offered an affable grin, his mustache twitching. "I was driving past and saw you and your car from the road. I wondered if you were okay." His grin widened. "I can see now you are."

"Yes. Ridge and I met up here a while ago. For...dinner. He was just dropping me off."

"Oh. Excuse me. Sorry if I interrupted."

"It's fine." Elena's confidence returned. "I was just leaving."

Oscar didn't move. His gaze narrowed on Ridge.

"We both were leaving," Ridge added, infusing a bite to his voice.

The standoff lasted another twenty seconds.

"Well, don't let me keep you," Oscar finally said. With a curt salute, he departed.

Ridge and Elena didn't talk until he'd vacated the parking lot.

Her expressive eyes met Ridge's. "Am I wrong, or did that whole encounter seem strange to you?"

"Very strange." He opened her car door. Once she was seated behind the steering wheel, he asked, "How well do you know him?"

"Not well." Elena buckled her seat belt. "Maybe I should do a little snooping."

"Be discreet," Ridge warned.

She reached for her door handle. "If I find anything interesting, I'll let you know."

Elena stood at the entrée table in the fellowship hall at church. She should have known better than to attend the winter picnic with Ridge. The hall had hummed with whispers when they entered. Elena could practically hear what people were saying. Two of Hillside Church's flock had found each other. She would hate disappointing them when the time came to confess that she and Ridge were pretending in order to divert suspicion.

She also hated lying. Did the end justify the means? She hoped the members and God would understand and forgive.

"That smells delicious."

Elena glanced behind her and smiled at old Mr. Harmon. "Do you like pozole?" She replaced the lid on her contribution to the lunch fare so it would stay warm.

"Indeed, I do. Please tell me you brought homemade tortillas to go with the soup."

"I'm sorry, no. Next time."

"Young Ridge Burnham is a fortunate man to be dating such a fine catch as yourself."

Elena cheeks grew warm, whether from Mr. Harmon's compliment or the reference to Ridge, she couldn't be sure.

"I don't know about that," she demurred.

"She's definitely a catch," Ridge said, joining her and the kindly gentleman. "Don't let her say differently."

"No need to convince me." Mr. Harmon winked. "Enjoy yourselves, you two."

"We will." Ridge placed a hand on Elena's shoulder.

She should have objected, but she didn't.

Every February, the church put on a winter picnic. The purpose of the event was to bring brightness to what was often a dreary time of year. The tables were covered with red-and-white-checkered cloths, and at the center of each sat an aluminum watering pot filled with white and yellow silk daisies. People had been encouraged to wear summer garb, and she saw an array of shorts, Hawaiian shirts and sundresses. The thermostat sat at a toasty seventy-six degrees, as opposed to the brisk fifty-eight outside.

Elena had dug out a pair of shorts and a neon green blouse. With her hair gathered in a ponytail, she did feel summery, especially standing next to Ridge in his "Fun in the Sun" T-shirt and flip flops.

They wandered over to the table that Jake, Gracie and the girls had claimed. There was no getting out of it. She and Ridge would have to sit with his family. Again. And this time it might be worse. Gracie continued to express her delight that her little brother was dating. Jake appeared less delighted. Much, much less.

Elena wondered if he'd give her any grief at the station. Probably—and mostly in retaliation because Oscar and the chief would give Jake grief. Jokingly, but not jokingly. Guys could be hard on each other.

"Hi, Uncle Ridge," the girls chorused when he and Elena sat down.

"Lindsey and Laney, say hi to Ms. Elena, too," Gracie prompted.

"Hi," they murmured, suddenly shy.

"Remember I told you she works with Daddy at the station?"

"Are you a sergeant deputy, too?" Lindsey asked.

"No." Elena smiled at the girl. "Just a plain old deputy."

"Is my daddy your boss?"

"Kind of. He's my immediate supervisor."

"What's the difference?"

Lindsey was pretty smart for a six-year-old.

"I can't fire her," Jake explained. "I can only tell her what to do."

Ouch. Elena hid her reaction by taking a sip of Ridge's excellent lemonade.

"Jake, be nice," Gracie chided. "Wouldn't you rather my brother date someone we like?"

"Who said I liked her?" He frowned, only to break into a grin when his wife elbowed him in the ribs. "Okay, okay. But how about we don't tell anyone at the station?"

Aha! He *was* worried about getting flak from the others.

They made small talk. Well, Gracie did most of the talking. When Elena snuck a glance at Ridge, his smile put her at ease.

From the front of the room, the minister called for everyone's attention. Midfifties and with a perpetually cheery countenance, he exuded warmth and compassion. "Welcome, welcome. It's wonderful to see so many familiar faces here today, and a few new ones. Glad our cloudy weather didn't keep you home."

After announcements, he said grace. The tables emptied one by one, and a line formed at the potluck buffet.

Lunch was a noisy, happy event. Everyone who got a bowl of Elena's pozole raved about it—Mr. Harmon more than anyone.

Elena patted his hand when he sat beside her. "Next time I make a pot, I'll bring you some."

"That would be splendid. I'm here most mornings."

He'd been given the title of custodian. For the most part,

he puttered around the church, vacuuming the sanctuary, offices and classrooms, making minor repairs and running errands. The job made the widower feel useful and filled his lonely hours. Elena had heard his children didn't visit much. She couldn't imagine it. He was such a nice, sweet man.

At the end of lunch, Jake and Ridge were roped into assisting with a plumbing malfunction in the kitchen. Elena pitched in with the cleanup, a chore that didn't take long. One good thing about potluck functions with paper plates and plastic-ware, there was little washing.

"Come with me." Gracie linked arms with Elena when they returned from taking out the trash, escorting her to an empty table. The girls played nearby with a friend from Sunday school. "Let's chat."

Elena's guard shot up. The other woman's tone hinted at more than a casual conversation. Should she tell Gracie that dating her brother was a ruse?

She and Gracie sat, and the other woman wasted no time getting to the heart of the matter.

"I know you're helping Ridge with the investigation of our dad's homicide."

The revelation took Elena aback. Seemed she didn't have to confess. "You do?"

Gracie laughed merrily. "I do now. I wasn't sure. Don't ever get into acting, Elena. You're not very convincing."

So much for three years in high school drama club. A waste of time, apparently.

"Ridge is younger than me," Gracie continued. "I saw more of the damage our dad's drinking did to our parents' marriage and how it changed our mom. She wasn't always angry and bitter."

"He mentioned that."

Gracie nodded. "Dad was a jovial drunk. Which is better than a mean drunk, for sure, but Ridge remembers Dad as this big, lovable man who took him prospecting in the mountains and horseback riding and taught him about raising cattle. He doesn't remember Dad missing birthdays and holidays because he was drinking at the bar, or our truck being repossessed because the monthly payment money went to bail him out of jail."

"I think he's aware of those things," Elena ventured.

"He is. Here." Gracie tapped her head. "In his heart, he still idolizes Dad. That's why he's always pushing the police to solve Dad's case. And why, since finding the gun and money, he began his own investigation. There are still people in town who believe Dad was inebriated and his death was an accident. Proving he was murdered would earn him people's sympathies rather than their scorn. That's important to Ridge."

"Perhaps Ridge feels that when people look down on or speak ill of his dad, it's a reflection of him."

"Oh, that's exactly what he feels. Which is one of the reasons he bails on relationships before they get serious."

This was the first Elena had heard about Ridge's past romances. She had no reason to feel discouraged, yet she did.

"We're not in a relationship," she blurted, as much for Gracie's benefit as her own. Though after her and Ridge's hug in the bank parking lot the other night, their pretend dating didn't feel so pretend to Elena.

"You could be. I can see he likes you and you like him. Which is why I'd hate to see you hurt."

"We hardly know each other."

"Maybe I shouldn't have said anything about his unwillingness to commit. Please don't think poorly of him." Gracie's expression pleaded for understanding. "He isn't a player or a bad guy. Deep down, he believes he doesn't bring enough to the table."

"That's...ridiculous."

"I agree. He's done well for himself. Retired from rodeoing with multiple world championship titles and money in the bank. He has every reason to be proud of himself. People respect him. But they also gossip about him. About us. Our dad, his drinking, his death. Ridge can't let go, and he's convinced he can't move on until he learns who killed Dad."

"Please don't take this the wrong way, Gracie." Elena chose her words carefully. "Is that how people feel, or how *you* feel?"

Rather than get angry, Gracie let her shoulders slump. "I won't say you're wrong, Elena. I want Ridge to let go of the past and move on. For many reasons. His safety. His peace of mind. His emotional well-being. And for mine. As long as he continues to search for answers, none of us can put what happened behind us."

Elena's heart went out to the other woman. She had experienced something similar when she lost her grandmother and then, barely a year later, her grandfather. She still grieved the loss.

Laying a hand on Gracie's arm, she said, "I'm sorry. Tragedy is ruthless and greedy. No one is immune to its clutches, and once it grabs hold, it doesn't let go."

"Maybe you can talk to Ridge?" Hope lit Gracie's eyes. "Convince him of the futility?"

"I doubt I can convince Ridge of anything. He's quite stubborn."

Gracie sighed again. "Yes, he is. Don't let that handsome face fool you." Her mood abruptly shifted. "I like the Ridge I see with you. I wouldn't mind if the two of you got serious. I'm just not sure that's possible."

Elena didn't have time to digest what Gracie told her before Ridge and Jake returned.

"Daddy, Daddy," Lindsey called. "Come see our drawings."

Jake stopped at the nearby table to inspect his daughters' artwork, compliment their talents and give them each a kiss on the top of the head. "That's the best picture of a horse I've ever seen."

"It's a dog," Laney said, insulted.

"You're right. My mistake." He tugged on her curls and then wandered over.

"Did you fix the garbage disposal?" Gracie asked as he dropped down beside her.

Ridge slid into the empty chair next to Elena and bumped shoulders with her as if they were indeed dating. Gracie's words about him bailing on previous girlfriends echoed in her mind.

"Ridge is the one who fixed it," Jake said. "Guess all those repairs at the ranch are paying off. His handyman skills are improving."

"That and his finding-money skills." Gracie's gaze scanned the group when her pun fell flat. "Okay, not funny?"

Jake cleared his throat and glanced at the girls before continuing in a lower voice. "I've been telling Elena she needs to steer clear of our troubles. I know. I was here when the cartel was active and the drug trafficking was at its peak. They're no one you want to mess with."

"He does know," Gracie chimed in. "When Jake first came to Ironwood Creek, he was young and fresh to the sheriff's department and determined to do his part cleaning up the town. He confronted more than one of the drug runners and was even shot once."

"Shot?" Elena blinked in surprise. "I had no idea."

"In the thigh, just a flesh wound. It wasn't serious." His demeanor changed. "But I realized what I was up against, and that I wouldn't win if I took on the cartel single-handedly."

"I was so scared." Gracie reached up and lovingly patted her husband's cheek. "I could've lost him."

"We're not taking on the cartel," Ridge said.

"You are," Jake insisted. "It's obvious. And they have long arms that still extend into Ironwood Creek. There's talk that if Sheriff Cochrane isn't reelected next year, his crack-down-on-crime program will lose its funding, and the cartel will return in full force."

Elena jerked upright. "Is that true? I haven't heard any rumors."

"Cochrane isn't a shoo-in."

"He's well-liked."

"Not by everyone," Jake said. "His programs, all of them, could be in jeopardy. That's what happens when leadership changes."

Unfortunately, he was right. And the thought bothered Elena. Had coming to Ironwood Creek been the right decision for her? While prepared to uphold the law, attempting to do that in a town under the thumb of a dangerous drug cartel hadn't been her plan.

God, is this the path You want me on? I need to know if I should keep helping Ridge and that investigating his dad's death is the right thing.

Her worries must have been reflected in her features, for Ridge reached for her hand beneath the table and gave her fingers a squeeze.

"Elena and I should get going," he said.

"Us, too." Gracie nodded at the girls. "Laney will need a nap after this."

Jake rose and stretched. "Me, too."

In the parking lot, Elena and Ridge said their goodbyes to his family and parted ways.

Alone at last, Elena asked, "Jake was shot? He never told me. I can't believe he didn't mention it when he was warning me to avoid you."

"He and Gracie were dating at the time. I was competing on the rodeo circuit."

"Getting shot is no small deal."

"It really wasn't serious. He was up and around in a week." They reached her car, where he continued. "I remember he got a commendation or an honor or something for being wounded in the line of duty. Of course, he milked it for all it was worth with Gracie. She waited on him hand and foot."

"Well, he was entitled." Elena pulled her coat closer around her to ward off the mild chill. "I've been shot at, but never hurt. It's scary."

He frowned. "I didn't mean to make light of his injury. He's a good deputy."

"He is," Elena agreed, giving credit where credit was due.

"What I remember most is the ceremony in front of town hall. I was in between rodeos and came home for it. Gracie was so proud. Sheriff Dempsey's predecessor presented Jake with the award. The mayor at the time and Olivia Gifford were on hand, too."

"The church bookkeeper?"

"Yeah. She used to work for the mayor back then. His administrative assistant, I think."

A lightbulb flickered to life in Elena's head. "Have you ever talked to her about your dad's homicide?"

"No. Why?"

"Because she worked for the mayor. She's bound to have information that didn't make it into public records."

Ridge flashed her a conspiratorial smile. "When are you free next?"

"Monday afternoon."

"That's great. Olivia always works on Monday, processing the collections from the day before."

This, thought Elena, was the answer to her earlier prayer; she was meant to be here and to keep helping Ridge. Why else would this lead appear?

SIX

Ridge and Elena had decided not to call ahead and give Olivia Gifford any warning. Elena's idea. It wasn't that they didn't trust the church bookkeeper, but Elena said people automatically got defensive when questioned, even in a casual situation. When caught unaware, they tended to reveal more. That had made sense to Ridge.

On their way down the hall, they ran into Mr. Harmon. He pushed a mop and bucket on wheels toward the restrooms.

"Afternoon, sir." Ridge nodded.

The elderly man broke into a toothy smile. "What brings you two here on a Monday afternoon?"

"Is Mrs. Gifford in her office?" Elena indicated the partially open door.

"You bet, as usual."

"Thank you." She touched Ridge on the arm.

He got the message. Move along and say nothing.

"You have a nice day, sir," Ridge told Mr. Harmon.

"Same to you." The wheels on the bucket squeaked as he pushed it across the tiled floor.

At the office door, Ridge knocked. Mrs. Gifford alternated days with the church secretary. They shared a desk, computer, printer and copy machine. The congregation wasn't so large that two offices were required.

"Hello," a lilting voice responded.

He pushed open the door. "Mrs. Gifford?"

"Ridge. Hello. Come in." Her expression showed surprise when Elena accompanied him. "Oh, you brought company."

"I hope we're not disturbing you."

"Not at all." She removed her reading glasses and set them on a bank bag in front of her. "Would you like a water? And there're some leftover cookies from Sunday school yesterday."

Ridge and Elena both declined and sat in the twin visitor chairs facing the desk. He guessed the bookkeeper to be sixty-plus, based on how long she'd been a member of the church. But her flawless complexion and trim figure gave the impression of a much younger woman. If Ridge believed his sister's claim, Mrs. Gifford had had "some work done" a few years ago during a supposed trip to Southern California. He didn't care one way or the other about the rumored plastic surgery. To each their own. If she had the money and preserving her good looks made her happy, who was he to criticize?

Her glance traveled from him to Elena and back again. Ridge got straight to the point, another of Elena's suggestions.

"I'm sure you heard I found a gun and strongbox of cash on my property last week."

"I did!" Her brows rose, disappearing beneath the fringe of her fashionably styled hair. "Isn't that something?"

"I believe they're connected to my dad's homicide. Chief Dempsey sent them to a lab in Tucson for testing. We're waiting on the results."

"Really!"

"I asked Elena to come with me today and offer her advice."

"Amateur sleuths. I love it." She covered her mouth with her hand and looked embarrassed. "I listen to some of those true crime podcasts. You know the ones. Promise you won't tell anyone. I would die. My husband is always making fun of me."

"We won't tell."

"We promise," Elena added.

Ridge noticed she sat quietly, listening and watching. Just

like she had that first day in his kitchen. Did Olivia referring to her as an amateur sleuth bother her? Ridge didn't think so.

"What have you found out?" the bookkeeper asked.

"Not much." He didn't mention the text Elena had received, the warning from Detective Darnelly or that he and Elena were followed. "That's the problem, which is why we're here. We're hoping you might provide some insight."

"Me?" She drew back, her hand dropping to rest above her heart.

"You worked for the mayor around the time my dad was killed."

Elena had been right. Instantly, Olivia's demeanor changed from friendly to wary.

"Yes, but what does that have to do with anything? Mayors aren't involved with police investigations."

"They do work together, though, right?" Ridge asked. "Mayors are kept abreast of investigations into local homicides."

"Yes," Olivia acquiesced. "From what I recall about your dad's case, however, there wasn't much to investigate. No witnesses or DNA. No legitimate leads."

At her dismissive tone, Ridge felt his irritation rising. He took a calming breath.

"I've read the police reports. Not much effort was put into the investigation. Maybe you heard or saw something while you were at the mayor's office."

"No, I didn't."

"Please. It's important."

Olivia shook her head. "I can't help you."

Ridge hated accepting defeat, but he saw no other option. For whatever reason, the bookkeeper refused to discuss her experiences. But then, Elena appealed to her in a voice both compassionate and pleading.

"Mrs. Gifford, I understand you lost your sister in an automobile accident when you were a teenager. The driver of the car that hit her fled the scene. They didn't find him for almost four months."

Olivia gasped. "How do you know that? I never talk about her."

Ridge wondered, too.

"You made a Christmas cactus donation in her memory. It was in the church program."

Ridge wondered if Elena had used her access to official records to research the accident.

Olivia's eyes filled with tears. "It was a terrible time for my family. Her death nearly destroyed us."

"I'm sorry to bring up such unhappy memories." Elena paused. "I imagine you and your family had unresolved feelings about what happened to your sister. Perhaps even some anger. Certainly, you suffered all those months you waited to learn who had caused the accident and were relieved when the person was taken into custody."

The other woman sniffed and snatched a tissue from the box on her desk. "I've forgiven the driver. That's the Christian thing to do."

"Which is very kind of you. There are people in your shoes who couldn't or wouldn't."

"I'm not sure what this has to do with Pete Burnham's death."

Ridge worried that Elena's tactic may have the opposite of its intended effect. Olivia seemed to be shutting down. They needed to win her over.

"Surely," Elena said, "you can understand how Ridge feels. To go all these years, having no idea what really happened to his dad and knowing the person responsible got away free and clear."

A small crack seemed to appear in Olivia's invisible armor. She released a wobbly breath.

"That must be hard."

"It is," he agreed.

She thought a long moment, her fingers fiddling with the stem of her reading glasses. At last, she raised her chin.

"I don't *know* for certain, but I did overhear some conversations. One-sided, mind you. Once, the mayor was on the phone with Ironwood Creek's then–deputy chief. I put the call through myself, so I know that for a fact. The mayor said something to the deputy chief about the Bisbee police pressuring the investigating detective to…" She squinted as if searching her memory. "Let the case rot. I'm pretty sure that's an exact quote."

A surge of excitement wended its way through Ridge. "Are you sure he was talking about my dad's homicide?"

"Yes. The mayor mentioned him by name."

"What else can you tell us?" He braced his hand on the desk. Elena sent him a don't-scare-her-off look, and he sat back in the chair. "Even the smallest detail would be helpful."

"I… I…"

"Please, Mrs. Gifford," Elena coaxed. "You'd be doing us a great service."

"I don't like to gossip about people behind their back."

"You're not gossiping. No one is accusing you of that. Not for one second."

After more fiddling with her reading glasses, she said, "I'm telling you this only because I think highly of you, Ridge, and your sister. Your mother, too. She did her best under difficult circumstances."

"I appreciate that, ma'am." He waited, anxiety gnawing at him.

"I suspected the mayor was taking a kickback from the cartel. There were phone calls that came into his office from rough-sounding individuals who were quite rude to me. And visitors who gave me the chills." She shivered. "They always came in with these canvas satchels and left without them. The mayor stayed late on those days. I'd think, how stupid and obvious. They didn't even try to hide what they were doing.

But I suppose the cartel had no fear. They ran this town and most of the people in it." She started to cry and dabbed at her nose with the tissue.

"Tell us about that," Elena said.

"You were young, Ridge. You probably don't remember."

"I used to watch the drug runners driving across our property."

"No one did a thing about it," Olivia continued, composing herself. "We were afraid of the cartel, and our sheriff's deputies."

"The deputies?"

This was news.

After a moment and another dabbing of the tissue, Olivia said, "They were on the cartel's payroll. If not willingly, then they were scared into compliance."

Like his dad, Ridge thought, remembering the stranger in the barn threatening his dad.

"Were local landowners also receiving kickbacks from the cartel?" he asked.

"Without a doubt," Olivia said. "Those were some lean times economically. Folks were hurting. Out of work or reduced hours. The mayor was under a great deal of pressure to respond. The cartel took advantage of that by offering money."

"To people like my dad."

"I'm afraid so, Ridge."

Old anger rose anew. "If my dad's involvement with the cartel was common knowledge, why did people insist he fell because he was drunk?"

Olivia spoke after a long pause. "Admitting the cartel murdered those who stood in their way was not only frightening, it risked incurring their wrath. Denial was safer. That's still true even today."

What if his dad had undergone a change of heart like the argument with the stranger implied? Ridge wondered. If Olivia was to be believed, the cartel would have sent an operative after him. It made sense.

"That's why I quit my job with the mayor." Olivia drew in a shaky breath. "I couldn't take it anymore. All the stress and worry. I didn't want to hear or witness something and then have to fear for my life."

"I don't blame you," Elena said.

"Did my mom know?" Ridge asked, wanting and not wanting to hear the answer.

Olivia faltered. "I... I can't say for certain. But I believe she did."

Pain tugged at his heart. Why hadn't she told him? He'd questioned her enough over the years.

"Did you ever hear of anyone called the Hawk?" Elena asked.

Olivia jerked and then tried to cover it by smoothing the front of her sweater. Ridge noticed. Elena, too. Her sideways glance telegraphed as much.

"No." Olivia feigned ignorance. "Is that a real name?"

"It is. And are you sure?" Elena pressed.

The bookkeeper stiffened, in either offense or avoidance of the subject. "I need to get back to work. I leave at three."

Ridge chose not to pressure her. She'd clearly made up her mind. Whatever she knew about the Hawk, she wasn't telling. Because of that same fear she mentioned earlier? Did Olivia believe, like Jake and Frank Darnelly, that the cartel was still active in Ironwood? Maybe she worried she'd said too much, and there would be repercussions.

"Thanks for your help, Mrs. Gifford." Ridge stood. He still had questions for her, but they would have to wait for another day.

Elena also rose. "See you on Sunday."

"Have a good week." The bookkeeper slipped on her reading glasses and returned her attention to the computer, effectively dismissing them.

* * *

Mentioning the Hawk had definitely touched a nerve with Olivia Gifford. As a deputy sheriff, Elena had questioned plenty of guilty people who lied about what they'd done. She didn't need to be an expert in reading body language to spot the obvious signs: a nervous twitch, a change in speech patterns, fidgeting, putting up walls and presenting false smiles. Olivia had exhibited all of those and more.

At the door, Elena paused before exiting the office. She couldn't bring herself to leave, not without making one last attempt. When Ridge gave her an inquiring glance, she offered a reassuring nod.

Turning back to face Olivia, she asked, "By the way, does anyone else in town know about the former mayor's alleged involvement with the cartel?"

Again, Olivia hedged. "Probably."

"Who?" Ridge demanded before Elena could get the question out.

Olivia firmed her lips into a flat line. Elena expected the bookkeeper to send her and Ridge packing. She was wrong, though. After a moment, Olivia answered.

"If I were to hazard a guess, Chief Dempsey. He was the sergeant deputy at Ironwood Creek station in those days. Before his promotion. He and the former chief were close." She held up her hand and twined her first and second fingers together. "If the former chief was on the take, rest assured Dempsey was either complicit or uninvolved, but keeping quiet about it. Protect the sinner and you are equally guilty of sin, isn't that what they say?"

The accusation hit Elena like a dunking in ice water. She'd gone back and forth on Chief Dempsey's involvement with the cartel, only to decide that, for all his gruffness and imperfections, he was an upstanding officer of the law. To have someone else accuse him of misconduct, if not out-and-out lawbreaking, forced a rush of air from her lungs. Ridge was equally struck by Olivia's proclamation, given his astonished expression.

"What happened to the former deputy chief?" Elena inquired in a tenuous voice.

"He resigned shortly after Pete Burnham's homicide and died rather suddenly."

"How?"

"Something to do with his heart." Olivia lifted a narrow shoulder. "Apparently, he had a previously undiagnosed condition."

That sounded rather convenient to Elena. Retiring soon after a local was killed and then suddenly dying?

No. She was letting her imagination run wild, fueled by her disarming conversation with Olivia.

"What about the former mayor?" she asked. "Does he still live in the area?"

Olivia shook her head, her manner brusque with impatience. "He retired and moved to Florida."

"Is he still alive?"

"I have no idea. He never kept in touch with anyone in Ironwood Creek."

"Okay. Thank you again, Mrs. Gifford." Elena could probably find out that information on her own. Just not at the station in case someone was tracking her activity on the computers.

Outside, in the hall, she put a finger to her lips, alerting Ridge not to talk until they were out of earshot. She wouldn't put it past the bookkeeper to jump out of her chair and attempt to listen at the door.

In the church lobby, they headed toward the double glass doors.

Ridge pushed on the lever, and they stepped outside. "I hate to say this, but I think she was hiding something."

"Agreed. She's heard of the Hawk, that's for sure."

"Don't you think it's coincidental the former deputy chief and mayor both left their jobs soon after my dad was killed?"

"Very. Especially since, according to Olivia, the mayor and perhaps the former chief were taking kickbacks."

"Did the cartel get rid of them?" Ridge asked.

"They may have left because they were targeted."

"A sudden heart attack and a previously undiagnosed condition? That sounds pretty fishy to me," Ridge said.

His thoughts mirrored her own. "There's no way we can prove anything," she said.

"Sounds like Olivia left her job in the nick of time."

"I'd have kept my mouth shut, too, if I was her. Three people have died over the years, including your dad. I'm surprised she didn't move to the other side of the country."

"What about Chief Dempsey? It sounds like he was involved."

Elena felt renewed shock as she and Ridge hurried across the concrete walkway toward the parking lot. Rain was in the forecast, and the temperature had dropped several degrees. She pulled her coat more tightly around her.

"That's a tough one," she said, still grappling with this new knowledge concerning her boss. "I respect the chief, and I like him. I hate entertaining the possibility that he's involved in any way. But he's one of the people who knew I was going to Bisbee the other day. And he could be tracking my activity on the station computer, though if he were, why would he have warned me about it?"

"What about Oscar Wentworth? Him just showing up the other night when we were in the bank parking lot? I didn't buy his story about driving by and seeing your car. Plus, his sedan looks an awful lot like the one that tailed us."

"I didn't buy it, either. And he's been at the station a long time. Part of that during the cartel's heyday."

"Did you ever find out anything more about him?"

"Yeah. He had a couple of personal judgments against him years ago for loans he defaulted on. They were eventually paid off."

"When?" Ridge asked.

"Right before Sheriff Cochrane was elected and launched his anti-crime campaign."

"Another coincidence?"

"They're adding up."

As they neared Elena's car, they heard Mr. Harmon hailing them. They turned and waited for the older man to catch up.

"I think you dropped these in the hallway." He held out a set of keys. "I found them outside Olivia's office."

Ridge patted his jacket pockets and then took the keys. "Thanks. I didn't realize I'd dropped them."

"You'd have figured it out."

"You saved me the trouble."

"Happy to oblige." Instead of leaving, he asked, "Did you get everything squared away with Olivia?"

Elena suspected Mr. Harmon was fishing for information. He wasn't so much a busybody as he was a bored old man. Not much went on in his life. Her and Ridge visiting the church bookkeeper had probably been the highlight of his day, if not the past few days.

"She was very helpful," Ridge said.

"She's a good person. Volunteering like she does."

"I thought the bookkeeper was a paid position," Ridge said. "Like the secretary."

"The secretary, yes. The bookkeeper, no. Olivia does the work for free."

"That's very generous of her," Elena added.

"She'd be the first to tell you she doesn't need the money." Mr. Harmon chuckled. He appeared in no hurry to get back, relishing the chance to chat with people. "And I reckon that's true. She never took another job after quitting the mayor's office. No need after she came into all that money."

Elena's ears pricked up. She hadn't heard this about the church bookkeeper. "What money?"

"Some relative died and left her a windfall." Mr. Harmon

winked. "That's how she paid for all those 'spa treatments,' if you catch my drift."

Evidently, the stories about her having a face lift and other procedures weren't mere rumors. Elena and Ridge exchanged glances. Were they thinking the same thing?

"I'd love to stay and chat longer," she told Mr. Harmon. "But I'm on duty in a couple of hours. I need to go home first and change."

"Of course, of course. Didn't mean to keep you. I've got to finish up here for the day." He gave them a wave before shuffling off, his gait stilted.

"Olivia came into a windfall right after leaving the mayor's office," Elena said to Ridge the moment they were alone.

"Is there a chance she was receiving a cut of whatever was in those satchels the cartel delivered to the mayor?"

"She was in a position to hear and see a lot. The cartel may have bought her silence."

Ridge looked uncertain. "If she was in on it, then why would she tell us as much as she did?"

"That's a good question." Elena met Ridge's gaze. "As is why didn't she leave town or have something untoward happen to her like the former mayor and chief?"

"She does know more than she's admitted."

"Absolutely," Elena agreed, mentally adding Olivia to her list of suspicious people to research.

"Let's meet again. At the ranch this time?"

"I'll call you later when I know my schedule for the next few days. Jake asked for personal time off tomorrow. We're scrambling to cover for him."

Ridge frowned. "Gracie didn't mention anything."

"He didn't say what for, and I didn't ask." In Elena's opinion, personal time off was just that. Personal.

"I'll wait to hear from you. But for now, we have a plan." Ridge squeezed her arm before walking briskly to his truck.

Elena climbed in behind the wheel, deliberating a moment

before starting the engine. Since coming to Ironwood Creek, she'd been worried about fitting in with the good old boys' club, being taken seriously and proving her worth.

Now, it seemed, she had something else to worry about. The possibility that the men she worked side by side with were accessories to murders, if not the ones who carried them out.

SEVEN

Elena wandered into her living room, cradling a cup of herbal tea and stifling a yawn. She should hit the sack. She'd been up all night on duty, responding to one call after the other with no downtime in between.

There'd been another theft at the Creekside Inn. This time, a room was broken into and ransacked. The guest admitted to not realizing her key card was missing. During the ninety minutes she spent having dinner with a friend at The Smoke Shack, the burglars—presumed to be the same two men from before, wearing hoodies and ski masks as revealed on security footage—had recovered her key card from where she dropped it in the parking lot and entered the room, stealing a pair of expensive earbuds, designer sunglasses, an electronic tablet, four hundred dollars in cash and several bottles of prescription drugs.

No, the guest hadn't availed herself of the complimentary room safe. No, she wouldn't make that mistake again. And, no, the manager hadn't the faintest idea how the burglars were casing the inn without being spotted.

Mere moments after Elena returned to the station, she'd been dispatched on another call. The cat lady's neighbor, a single mom, had reported a prowler in her backyard. She was home alone with her small children, and she was nervous. When Elena arrived, she'd heard the dog with the curly hair barking furiously from inside the house. Obtaining the mother's consent, she'd checked the entire yard, her flashlight beam zigzagging across the lawn. Near the fence line, she discovered a paper bag. Opening it up, she grimaced at the offensive smell and averted her face before retching. The bag was filled with rancid meat.

She suspected the cat lady of attempting to poison the dog but, without proof, had made no outright accusations. The mom instantly came to the same conclusion on her own and had burst into tears. All Elena could do was advise her to repair the fence, install security measures and keep her dog inside as much as possible.

"I'll talk to my ex-husband," she'd said. "See if he will help."

"If not," Elena had told her, "call me. My number's on that card. Hillside Church has a community assistance program run by volunteers."

The mom had cried again and hugged Elena.

"Good fences make good neighbors," she'd said, right before her radio went off and she was driving to the next call—reported trespassers in the abandoned pecan grove. After the recent rain, the grove was a mud pile. Elena had managed to get covered in grime from head to toe.

When she arrived home at 7:00 a.m., she'd immediately jumped into the shower. The hot water had felt wonderful and also revived her. She needed to sleep; she'd be reporting for duty at six this evening. But she also needed to wind down first; otherwise, she'd toss and turn. The tea would make her drowsy. So would reading a book or magazine, especially in bed. Except Elena's mind refused to stop churning.

She'd been thinking about Ridge and their conversation with Olivia every free minute since they'd left the church. Also, what Mr. Harmon had said. On the surface, the facts of the bookkeeper resigning her job with the mayor and then coming into a substantial amount of money from a distant relative had nothing to do with each other. Elena's gut insisted differently.

Too many things had happened in the wake of Pete Burnham's death to write them all off as coincidences. Add to that Ridge finding the gun and money. What was the common thread? Or person? There had to be one.

Olivia Gifford had lived in Ironwood Creek during the peak of the cartel's drug trafficking. She'd also worked for the mayor, who in all likelihood had received kickbacks from the cartel, and she had remained in town when others had fled or died under mysterious circumstances. Wasn't she worried she'd seen too much and was at risk?

Elena needed to learn more about the bookkeeper. Then, she and Ridge could visit her again with additional hard-hitting questions. Elena knew they wouldn't catch her unaware this time. She'd clam up the instant they stepped into her office. Because of that, a plan was in order.

There was that word again. *Plan.* She and Ridge were making them frequently of late.

She sat down at her dining table and booted up her laptop. She sipped her tea and stared out the glass patio door at the nearby mountains. Ridge had a similar view of the same mountains from his ranch. What were the chances he was enjoying a morning beverage and staring at their rounded peaks?

Enough, she told herself. *Stop relating every thought and action to him.*

Great view aside, she did like this apartment. Being on the first floor was a big plus. Rather than a balcony, she had a patio. On nice days, she sat in her chaise longue and watched the wildlife through the wrought-iron fence surrounding the complex. She frequently saw quail, rabbits and lizards, and a pair of bonded owls lived in the nearby stand of saguaro cacti. She didn't even mind the periodic coyote and javelina who visited, mostly at night.

If Elena wanted, she could exit through a gate and access

a network of walking trails in the ten-acre natural area adjacent to the complex. On her days off, sometimes she hiked or jogged the trails, along with her neighbors, many with their dogs.

Her dad was less fond of her proximity to the natural area, citing a security risk. Elena would kiss him on the cheek, count her blessings that she had parents who loved and cared for her, and then assure him that, along with her state-of-the-art locks, the apartment complex utilized high-tech cameras and employed a security service who patrolled every four hours.

Her argument had made no difference. Her dad purchased and installed a home security system for her that included cameras mounted outside her front and patio doors. Elena checked them regularly from the app on her phone and received notifications whenever movement was detected.

While it was on her mind, she glanced at the app on her phone. No alerts during the night while she'd been gone.

She then returned to her laptop and checked her inbox. Scanning the senders and subject lines of incoming emails, she answered a few and decided the rest could wait. Opening a search engine, she typed in Olivia Gifford's name. The results were mostly links to church and civic activities, nothing out of the ordinary. Olivia had served for a few years on the town council after leaving her job at the mayor's office. Not unusual for someone with a strong interest in town politics.

Elena clicked through various links, discovering an old photograph of Olivia at a fundraising dinner. She stood alongside her former boss, the mayor. Also included in the photo were the then chief of police and a man identified as Ironwood Creek business entrepreneur Marcus Rivera. Elena leaned closer to the laptop screen and scrutinized the photo. Did secretaries usually attend fundraising dinners? Perhaps Olivia had gone with her husband, but he hadn't been included in the photo. The mayor's wife wasn't in the photo, either.

Something in the photo suddenly caught Elena's eye, and she

squinted, only to draw back. Was that a young Chief Dempsey standing behind the mayor? She looked again. It *was* him. He would have been the sergeant deputy in those days.

She read the accompanying article. It was neither long nor informative. A fluff piece for the paper. But who was this Marcus Rivera?

A search of him revealed almost nothing. Elena found his name listed as the chairman of M.R. Investments, Inc., a company that operated about twenty-five years ago, then seemed to disappear fifteen years ago. She didn't have the experience or resources to learn more.

She next did what any investigator would—she scoured social media. Olivia had the kind of presence you'd expect from someone with children and grandchildren and who took annual vacations. Lots of posts about birthdays and holidays and trips. Elena quit skimming her pages after ten minutes. She found absolutely zero on Marcus Rivera. At least, no Marcus Rivera that could be the same man who'd attended the fundraising dinner.

Who was he, and what role had he played in Ironwood Creek's unsavory history? She considered asking Chief Dempsey. He'd been photographed with Marcus Rivera and might know more about the local businessman. Olivia Gifford no doubt did. But would she just clam up again if asked?

When Elena's phone abruptly rang, she gave a start. Her nervous reaction turned into a smile when she read Ridge's name on the display.

"Hi, how you doing?" she asked, leaning back in her chair.

"I was afraid I might wake you."

She liked the warm tone of his voice when he talked to her. "I'm heading to bed soon. I got sidetracked. Researching Olivia online."

"Find anything interesting?"

"Maybe." She told him about the old photo at the fundraiser dinner and Marcus Rivera. "Ever hear of him or M.R. Investments, Inc.?"

"Not that I recall. I was a kid at the time. If anyone mentioned him, it would have gone in one ear and out the other."

"What about your mom or sister? Maybe you could ask them if they ever heard of the Hawk."

"I will."

Elena's gaze drifted to her laptop. Did Ridge have a social media account? Gracie probably did. And she'd have pictures of Ridge.

Elena refused to type in either his or Gracie's name. She would not be that kind of person.

"We should also ask Olivia about this Marcus Rivera," Ridge said.

"Agreed." Elena let out a breath, glad to be back on track. "I also have a friend from the Maricopa County Sheriff's Department, Phoenix station, who has much better computer skills than me and owes me a favor."

"Okay. And I can pump Jake for information," Ridge offered. "He was around in those days. I just need to figure out a way to work it into conversation without alerting him."

"That won't be easy."

They discussed more strategy before deciding to meet at Ridge's ranch the following afternoon at four. Elena would be off work and able to catch six-ish hours of sleep after her shift and before leaving for Ridge's. That would also allow her time to call her friend from her old job in Phoenix.

"I'll make dinner," Ridge said. "In my brand-new kitchen. Save you the trouble."

"You don't need to do that." Dinner sounded a lot like a date to Elena. As had breakfast at the café and the winter picnic.

"No trouble. I'll just throw together a pot of chili and a pan of cornbread."

"Throw together?"

"That didn't sound appealing." He laughed. "It'll be edible, I promise."

She was about to comment when her phone buzzed with a notification from her security system. There was motion on her patio. She opened the app and saw an indistinguishable shape moving through the vicinity of her shadowed patio area.

"Ridge, I've got to go."

"What's wrong?"

"Probably nothing. My security system giving me a notice. I'm going to have to look."

"Elena." Alarm filled his voice. "I'll stay on the line with you."

She decided not to argue. "Okay."

Grabbing a jacket hanging from a hook on the wall, she stuffed the phone in her pocket then started for the Arcadia door, her heart racing.

Outside, she found an empty patio and saw nothing in either direction. Not so much as a spider climbing the patio wall.

"Elena?" Ridge's voice called to her from her pocket.

She took out the phone. "Yeah. I'm here. All's clear. Hold on while I check the app."

Sitting on the chaise lounge, she watched her phone screen, studying the dark shape rolling by. It could be a person crouched over. It could also be a large plastic trash bag floating on the wind. A big black dog. She rewatched the footage twice. At this time of morning, her west-facing patio lay in shadows. Between that and the black-and-white video, there was just no telling what had traveled past.

"I don't know what it is," she told Ridge and pushed to her feet. "I'll look again later when I'm not sleep-deprived."

"Are you sure you're going to be okay?"

"I'm sure." She went back inside and engaged her locks. She'd also sleep with her gun on her bedside nightstand rather than in the safe. "I have an alarm system."

"Call me when you wake up."

"I will." His concern for her brought a smile to her face. "And I'll see you tomorrow."

They disconnected, and Elena made for her bedroom. At the last second, she remembered her laptop. She'd left it on and with several tabs open, including her social media account.

When she leaned over the computer, she noticed a small box in the corner of her screen. Someone had sent her a direct message. Elena didn't recognize the sender's obscure name or the tiny cartoon character avatar and was about to delete the message when she flashed back on the threatening text she'd received. She clicked open and felt her pulse kick into overdrive as she read the sender's message.

Back off now or you and your family will regret it.

"Sorry, kiddo," Trudy said. "Wish I could be more help."

"Me, too." Elena sat at her dining table and rubbed her temples. "But I appreciate you trying."

"Without an IP address, it's hard to find out who's behind a fake social media account. And now that the person who sent the message has deleted the account, you're going to need a friend in the FBI rather than the sheriff's department to trace it."

Her former coworker and mentor from the Phoenix Sheriff's Department had done her best to assist Elena in identifying the person behind the threatening direct message. She'd walked Elena through the steps over the phone, but to no avail. The account had disappeared into cyberspace.

"Have you told your friend Ridge yet?" Trudy asked.

"Yes. About the object picked up by my motion detector. Not the direct message. Not yet." She swallowed. "I will. Today."

"You'd better."

"He's worried, even though I downplayed it." Elena had filled her in on Ridge and their relationship at the start of their phone call. "I said it was just a trash bag."

"He's right to be worried. This is the second threat you received."

"I was hoping to have good news to tell him after we talked."

"And now that you don't?"

"My guess is he'll go a little off the deep end."

"Elena, this person specifically mentioned your family. Please tell me you alerted them. They need to be on the lookout."

"I called my dad."

"That's a relief. What did he say?"

"You've met him. He wants me to quit my job here, move back home and stay barricaded in my old room for a year."

"Maybe you should. This is serious business."

"You're right." She sighed. "Dad was also understanding. He said he'd want to help out a friend, too, if he was in my shoes. That it's the Christian thing to do."

"I agree—to a point. As long as it doesn't endanger you or anyone else."

"The thing is," Elena said, "I feel sorry for Ridge. Pete Burnham was likely killed to silence him or prevent him from testifying against someone high up in local government."

"You don't want the same thing to happen to you and Ridge," Trudy warned.

"No, but I also hate the idea of a killer getting away scot-free. Not once but three times." She'd told her friend about the other unsolved homicides. "There was a serious criminal element in Ironwood Creek at one time that got away with a lot. They should be exposed."

"Be realistic. They're long gone. You said yourself you've seen no evidence of them now, which means someone else is behind these messages."

She was sure it was someone who used to be in cahoots with the cartel. Elena mentally ran through her list. Olivia Gifford. Chief Dempsey. Oscar. Jake. Marcus Rivera. The man who'd argued with Ridge's dad. Who else? Who hadn't they thought of yet?

"I have to find out who's sending me those threatening messages."

"Don't be foolish, Elena. No need to risk your life and that of your family. Tell Ridge about this latest message and then drop out of the investigation. If he wants to continue on his own, that's his business."

"I'm just trying to help a friend get the answers he deserves."

"A friend or a *boyfriend*?"

"It's not like that," Elena insisted, even as she remembered the sensation of Ridge's arms around her during their brief hug and the warm timbre of his voice on the phone. "You know me. Career first above all else."

"I used to say that." Trudy's voice became wistful. "Until I met Richard and was convinced otherwise. You know it's possible to have both a career and a personal life."

"Two step-kids. One of your own. A demanding job. A mother-in-law with health issues. I honestly don't know how you do it."

"A lot of love and a lot of patience."

And a lot of sacrifices, thought Elena. She'd seen that first-hand. Her mother and grandmother had given up so much to run the family in order that their husbands could dedicate themselves to their jobs. College. Travel. Friendships. Her mother had abandoned a job she loved when she became pregnant with Elena's older sister.

Elena was certain her mother didn't regret a single decision she'd made or a moment of her life. But could Elena ask the same of her future spouse? To give up something they loved for her and her career?

Ridge had a ranch and a dream of raising cattle. Would he be willing to sell and move if a transfer benefited her? Stay home with the children? Not object to her intense and ever-changing hours? Sympathize with and be supportive of her bad mood when she had a grueling day? It was a lot to expect and not the life for everyone.

There was also the other question to consider. Would she be willing to make sacrifices for her husband? Because isn't that what married people did? Give and take?

It was all so complicated. Elena wanted what her friend Trudy had achieved. A serious, loving relationship and a family. When the time was right, she prayed she'd meet the right person and that the circumstances would fall into place.

She thought again of Ridge. To be honest, she had no idea what he was looking for down the road. Assuming he even wanted a wife and family, how long would he be willing to wait for the right woman? More than likely, once she finished helping him with his dad's homicide—which might be today after he learned about this latest message—they'd go back to being acquaintances at church. The idea of that caused a small prick of pain.

Elena glanced at the time on her phone. She needed to hurry. She was supposed to be at the Burnham ranch in less than an hour. "Any chance we can meet for coffee or lunch next time I'm in Phoenix?"

"I'd love nothing better," Trudy said. "And if you need anything else, give me a holler."

"Thanks."

Elena went to her bedroom and studied the contents of her closet. What did one wear to a strategy session that might turn into a not-seeing-each-other-again get-together? Jeans, she decided. And a sweater.

She and Ridge had talked on the phone several times since yesterday morning when her security camera had detected motion. Elena replayed the events in her head. She'd been distracted by a motion notification on her phone app. Then, when she returned to her computer a few minutes later, a threatening message awaited her.

The events were too coincidental for her comfort level. But how could the person who sent the message know she'd be away from her computer unless they were the cause of the distraction? Then again, what did it matter if she was at her computer when the message arrived?

At Ridge's insistence, she'd gone to the apartment complex office and spoken to the assistant manager. The woman checked with the security company who serviced the complex. Their guard reported no suspicious activity at the time Elena's phone alerted her or all week, for that matter. She was the only resident to contact the office. Additionally, a review of the surveillance video showed nothing of concern.

"Could have been a tumbleweed," the assistant manager had suggested. "Or a raven. They can be such pests. Or a drone. They're popular now."

At least it wasn't a person. That was what had mattered to Elena.

Regardless, Trudy was right. Maybe Elena should tell Ridge about the new message and take a step back from the investigation into his dad's death. Her own safety aside, she refused to put her family in jeopardy. Except, quitting on a friend didn't come easy for her. That do-gooder personality again.

As she brushed her hair, she contemplated a way to continue helping Ridge that didn't make the cartel—or whoever was menacing her—nervous. The two of them could discuss it over dinner.

Elena checked her rearview mirror every couple of minutes during the drive. As she pulled into the Burnham Ranch, she was reminded of her visit there the day Ridge had found the gun and strongbox. They were still awaiting test results from the lab. Sage had been right, requesting the tests be expedited had made no difference.

Additionally, Elena had yet to find the right moment to speak to the chief about the photo from the fundraiser and Marcus Rivera. He'd either been busy with paperwork, on the phone, going over the schedule with Sage, or not at the station the same time as Elena.

In light of the threatening social media message, she considered not speaking to the chief. He may have been involved with the cartel and Pete Burnham's murder, much as she disliked the notion.

Ridge had texted her before she left her apartment, telling her to come directly to the barn when she arrived. She'd assumed he was working on repairs or renovations. She parked in front of the house and walked over to the barn, noting some improvements in the two weeks since her last visit. The pasture and round pen fencing had received a fresh coat of white paint. Missing shingles and side panels on the barn had been replaced, and a rooster weathervane perched atop the roof ridge, transforming the structure from rundown to quaint.

Ridge had been busy. Elena was impressed.

Nearing the large opening, she called, "Hello."

"In here."

She entered the barn, pausing a moment to let her eyes adjust to the dim lighting. The interior appeared noticeably tidier. Junk had been hauled away. The barn floor was swept clean and thick rubber mats lay along the center aisle. Tools hung from pegs on the walls, grouped by type. The storage room door sat ajar, revealing a pair of racks holding saddles, bridles and other horse tack.

The sweet smell of straw filled the air. It came, she realized, from several bales stacked alongside the row of stalls.

"I've got something to show you." Ridge beckoned her from where he stood in front of a stall.

The seriousness of his tone turned her curiosity into concern. Had he found something, perhaps the gold chain?

"Ridge, what is it?"

"You'll have to come here and see for yourself."

Ridge watched as Elena walked slowly toward him, well aware he was causing her unnecessary anxiety. Her features, usually controlled, telegraphed her anxiety. But he couldn't resist having fun with her. They were always so serious.

"Did you find the gold chain?" she asked, approaching the stall.

"I wish. But not yet." He hadn't given up hope. "Something else. It seems I've acquired some livestock."

"Cattle?" Her worry transformed into excitement. "You said you were going to get some once the ranch was in shape. I saw the improvements on my way in."

"Not cattle. Think smaller."

"Calves?"

"Wrong animal. And there's only one."

"Ridge." She groaned with frustration and then joined him at the stall. Peering over the door, she let out a surprised gasp. "Oh, my goodness. A miniature donkey. How cute."

"Meet Minnie Pearl." He gestured to the diminutive gray animal standing amid an abundance of fresh straw. "She's going to be staying with me for a while."

"Minnie Pearl?"

"I'm told she's named after an old-time comedienne. Apparently, the real-life Minnie Pearl used to greet audiences with a loud howdy when she stepped on stage. And this Minnie Pearl is not only a miniature donkey, she has a bray that will rattle your bones. Wait until you hear her."

Elena laughed, a sound Ridge had grown fond of hearing.

"Come on." He unlatched the door. "She's friendly."

Elena followed him into the stall. Minnie Pearl lifted her disproportionately large head in a plea for attention. Elena obliged and scratched the donkey between the ears. Minnie Pearl closed her eyes in contentment.

"Aren't you a sweetheart," Elena crooned. When she stopped scratching, Minnie Pearl nudged her for more. "And tiny."

"She's just eight hands." Ridge removed a piece of carrot from his jacket pocket and passed it to Elena. "Here. Give her this."

"What's eight hands?"

"Hands are how equine height is measured. An average horse is fifteen or sixteen hands. So she's half their height."

"Pony size."

Minnie Pearl gobbled the carrot, crunching loudly.

"She wants more," Elena said.

"Sorry, girl." Ridge patted her neck. "That was the last."

Stamping a delicate hoof, Minnie Pearl drew back, opened her mouth and emitted a high-pitched, ear-splitting sound that gained volume as it reverberated off the barn walls.

Elena stared in shock. "Did that big sound really just come out of her?"

"Now you know how she got her name."

"She's too small for you to ride. What are you going to do with her?"

Ridge gave Minnie Pearl another pat. "She belonged to an old rodeo buddy of mine. He was in a bind and couldn't keep her anymore. I said I'd take her in and try to find her a home." He checked the waterer, which he'd repaired before Minnie Pearl's arrival. It had been fifteen years since the stall was last occupied. "Who knows, I may keep her. She's doesn't eat much, and I kind of like having something else on this ranch besides me. I'm tired of talking to myself."

"Not that you aren't good company, but won't she get lonely in this big barn by herself?"

"I was thinking of getting a horse, though horses and donkeys don't always get along." He rubbed a knuckle along his chin. "I should probably adopt a wild burro or two at the Bureau of Land Management auction next month. They never have enough homes for the hundreds they round up every year."

"Seriously, burros? I thought you wanted to raise cattle."

"I can do both."

She smiled tenderly at him. "You have a soft heart."

"Don't tell anybody."

"Your secret's safe with me." She returned to scratching

Minnie Pearl between the ears. "When I was a little girl, I dreamed of owning a horse. Read every Walter Farley and Marguerite Henry book ever published."

Ridge smiled and shifted, closing the distance between them. "I could teach you to ride if you're interested."

She raised her wide, dark eyes to his. Ridge lost himself in their brown depths.

"But you don't have any horses," she said. "Not yet."

"I could borrow a pair. I know plenty of people I could ask."

"Um, we'll see."

"We won't always be investigating my dad's homicide. If you're worried about there being a conflict of interest..."

His gaze connected with hers and held. Ridge knew there was no reason for them to continue standing there in the stall. She'd come to the ranch so they could talk strategy. Only right now, standing close to Elena, that seemed like a million miles away.

"Ridge." The hesitancy remained.

He steeled his resolve. His intention wasn't to pressure her, but rather convince her of his sincerity.

"I won't lie," he said. "I'd like to spend more time with you and get to know you better. For real, not as some cover story. Horseback riding strikes me as a good way to accomplish that. If we both decide we like each other, we can go from there."

She didn't say yes. She didn't say no, either, which gave him the confidence to continue.

"But if that were to happen," he said, "there are some things you need to know about me first."

"That sounds ominous."

"Just full disclosure."

"Ah. I see."

He opened the stall door. Elena couldn't leave without giving the donkey's fluffy head a final scratching. He closed the stall door quickly before Minnie Pearl escaped and slid the latch in place. He'd come back later and give her some grain.

He and Elena ambled over to an old metal folding chair near the tools. Ridge gestured for Elena to sit, and he flipped over a plastic bucket to use as a stool.

"I wasn't always a believer," he began as they got settled. "We attended church when I was a kid, but after my dad was killed, well, Mom had a falling out with God, I suppose you could say, and we stopped going. Honestly, I didn't mind and spent my Sundays practicing roping and, later, bull riding."

"I can see how losing your dad in such a tragic way caused your mom to struggle with her faith."

"When I started rodeoing professionally, a few of the guys introduced me to the Cowboy Church. I attended at first only because a good friend was trampled by a bronc and seriously injured. He was in the hospital for days, hanging on by a thread. A bunch of us went to a Cowboy Church service and prayed for him. I tagged along just to be supportive. The next morning, my friend was upgraded from critical to stable. I told myself the power of prayer couldn't have accomplished such an amazing turnaround. But the possibility intrigued me, and I attended another service the following week in a different town. A year later, I became a member of Cowboy Church."

Elena's features softened. "That's an incredible story."

"When I moved back to the ranch, I started going to Hillside, which is where I went as a kid. They welcomed me as if I'd never left."

"They welcomed me as if I'd always belonged."

"Faith is an important part of my life."

"Mine, too," she said.

"I'd hoped it might repair the rift between my mom and me. That if I believed hard enough, we'd find common ground on which to build." His chest grew tight with emotion. "Hasn't happened."

Elena reached out and touched his arm, the gesture saying more than words could.

"My dad's choices hurt my mom and disappointed her and

sucked every ounce of joy out of her. She hasn't forgiven him, and she doesn't understand how I have. Me living here has stirred up a lot of unpleasant memories for her."

"You said she married a great guy."

"She did. Ben is perfect for her. She has every reason to be content—a good husband, two beautiful granddaughters, and Gracie and I are doing all right for ourselves. But Mom struggles to let go of the past." He tried to chuckle. "I inherited that from her."

"I'm not sure learning what happened to your dad is the same as refusing to let go of the past. You're seeking justice."

"You work in law enforcement. You understand that. Not everyone else does."

"I understand, but not because of my job." Elena swallowed, her thoughts appearing to turn inward. "My grandmother was killed three years ago."

He reached for her arm and squeezed it. "I'm so sorry."

"She was a wonderful person. She was kind and gentle and good, and I loved her to pieces. One night, she was walking the dog when she was attacked and beaten. In her own quiet neighborhood. She didn't survive her injuries. Her assailant wasn't found for seven months, until he attacked another person. That time, he was caught. DNA evidence connected him to my grandmother's assault. Three days after he was sentenced, my grandpa died, I believe from a broken heart. It was the worst time of my life."

Ridge longed to pull her to her feet and into a hug. He'd suspected she'd suffered a grave loss, and now he had confirmation.

"Thankfully, the second victim survived," Elena continued, her voice steely. "The assailant was homeless and a drug addict. It took a long time for me to forgive him. I wasn't sure I could. Then, later, we learned about his own sad family history. Our family pastor counseled us on the power of forgiveness. I was finally able to let go of my anger." She paused.

Inhaled. "So, I get how your mom feels about your dad. Loss can be an open wound that never heals."

Ridge studied Elena with new eyes.

"You're amazing. Thank you for teaching me that I should be more tolerant of my mom. And for sharing your story. That couldn't have been easy."

"I always wanted to go into law enforcement like my dad and grandfather. I didn't grasp how truly important the work is until my grandmother's attacker was on the loose those many months. Going the rest of my life without ever knowing, without closure, I can't... I can't imagine what you've gone through."

The bond Ridge had felt with her strengthened tenfold. They were a lot alike, especially in the ways that counted. Without much effort, she could win his heart.

"I tell myself the timing's wrong for me to date." He leaned in, took a lock of her hair and twirled it between his fingers. "That the ranch comes first."

"I tell myself that, too." She leaned in ever so slightly. "My career comes first."

He nodded and tucked the hair behind her ear. "Have you ever asked yourself why God brought us together, if the timing wasn't right for either of us? He could be telling us something. Maybe we should listen."

"What would that be?" Her words came out on a whisper.

"That our paths aren't meant to merely cross, but converge?" He hurried on before she could protest. "I like you, Elena. And I think you like me. We may be pretending to date, but there have been moments when it felt real to me. Moments, if I'm to be honest, when I wanted it to be real."

"I enjoy being with you, too."

He smiled. "Not just when we're crime-fighting?"

"What if God brought us together so that we could learn who killed your dad, not to date?"

"He could have more than one reason in mind."

"You're an optimist, Ridge, as well as a softie."

"There's always one way we can find out."

"How's that?" she asked.

"This."

He leaned in and brushed his lips across hers.

EIGHT

Elena hesitated for only a moment before letting go and responding to Ridge's oh-so-wonderful kiss. When he cupped her cheek with his palm, she melted into him as naturally as if this moment was always meant to be. And perhaps it was.

Time slowed. It may have stopped altogether. She knew she wanted their kiss to last…and last.

Eventually, they drew apart. Ridge stroked her jawline with his thumb before letting his hand drop.

"I don't regret that. I hope you don't, either."

"Not in the least."

He smiled, his gaze roving over her face. "Tell me there's a chance for us."

Elena sat back in the chair, reality returning with an unwelcome rush of cool air filling the empty space between them. She didn't like that, much preferring the warmth when they inhabited each other's personal space.

"What's wrong?" Ridge asked, his demeanor changing when she didn't immediately answer.

She hated causing him distress and shouldn't have waited to mention the threatening message. Minnie Pearl had been a temporary distraction, but not an excuse.

"There's something you need to know," she said, gathering her resolve. "Something I should have told you when I first arrived. Before you…before *we* kissed."

"What happened?"

She sighed. This was way harder than she'd anticipated. She'd liked their kiss, liked the prospect of them dating one day in the future. That would all end in the next few minutes.

"Elena. Tell me."

"I received another message, right after I hung up from talking to you."

"And you didn't tell me?" Storm clouds darkened his features. "What kind of message?"

"It was another threat, Ridge. This one against my family."

"Good Lord. Are you all right? Are they? What did the message say?"

"'Back off now or you and your family will regret it.'" The fear she'd been holding inside uncoiled. Here was the reason she'd avoided mentioning the message to Ridge. Then she'd have to admit how much it had shaken her.

"Is everyone okay?" he repeated.

"Yes. I called my dad right away. He and the family are taking precautions. Actually, he's handling the news better than I expected. That could change once it sinks in." She'd spoken to her family again this evening. "He knows the drill. He's received threats before, once when he arrested a dangerous gang member leader."

"That doesn't minimize the threat."

"No. Of course not. They're getting a hotel room for a couple nights."

"I'm glad to hear that." Ridge took hold of Elena's hand. "Are you okay?"

His concern touched her, and she found herself opening up to him. "I'm scared, at least a little. I'm mostly angry. I don't like being threatened, and I hate that my privacy has been invaded." She hated feeling vulnerable worst of all.

"What did the chief say?"

"I haven't told him yet."

"Elena! Why not? You and your family are in danger."

"I'll tell him when I report for duty tonight. He's going to advise me to inform admin and call the police like the last time."

"Which you should."

"We're not going to be able to trace the sender of the message. It was a DM on social media and the sender's account has already been deleted. There isn't much they or anyone can do. It's frustrating. And what if the chief is involved?" That concern, as much as her conviction that nothing would be done, had her waiting.

"If he is involved, you don't want him thinking you suspect him. Act normally. Tell him about the message and write up a report."

"Okay. Good idea. I will."

"You shouldn't be alone." His tone softened. "Do you have a friend who can stay with you? Or maybe you should get a hotel room like your parents. One in another town a hundred miles away."

"My dad suggested that, too. I'm considering it, but I hate the idea of hiding."

"Consider it hard, Elena. This is the second threat you've received."

"Yes, but I'm convinced whoever is sending me messages is using me to get to you. They believe, because I'm a woman, I'll frighten more easily, and you'll give up investigating your dad's homicide to protect me."

"They're not wrong, at least about the last part."

"We can't let them win," Elena argued.

"Oh yes, we can," he insisted. "Your safety and your family's are too important."

"Your dad deserves justice."

"This isn't your battle to fight."

She changed tactics. "What if we figure out a discreet way to keep investigating?"

The corners of his mouth rose in a reluctant smile. "Do you ever give up?"

"We're onto something," she insisted. "We just don't know yet what that is or how everything relates to your dad's homicide."

He closed his eyes and released a long breath. "You said the sender of the message can't be traced?"

"I called a former coworker of mine in Phoenix from the Maricopa County Sheriff's Department. She's a tech whiz." Elena explained how Trudy had walked her through the process of tracking the message's origin. "We couldn't find anything."

"It has to be the same person who sent you the text. Nothing else makes sense."

"How do they know what we're up to?" Elena rubbed her palms along the tops of her thighs, trying to release her pent-up energy. "That's what really bugs me. Even if someone close to me is keeping tabs, I haven't said anything to anybody. Have you?"

Ridge shook his head.

"I've been thinking. We can—"

"You're done helping me," Ridge said firmly.

She pretended not to hear him. "I should still talk to the chief about that fundraising photo. Marcus Rivera was involved with the cartel. I have no doubt. And the chief could confirm that. He was at the event."

"What if he's the one keeping tabs on you? You just said you don't trust him."

"I don't trust him, but I'm sure he holds the answers. He may not have been involved in your dad's homicide or with the cartel, despite what Olivia Gifford says, but he knows things. He was sergeant deputy under the previous corrupt chief. And we know for sure that *he* was in cahoots with the mayor and the cartel."

"Assuming Olivia wasn't lying to protect herself."

She shook her head. "I don't think she was. Not about the former chief and mayor. I watched her carefully. She was genuinely distraught when she described cartel members visiting the mayor."

Ridge stood. "I'll talk to the chief myself and figure out a way to continue investigating on my own."

"He won't tell you anything."

"Fine, but Jake might."

Elena also stood. "He doesn't want you involved any more than he wants me to be."

"He'll be more open if he thinks you and I aren't working together anymore."

"Maybe not. He wants you to stop pressuring the police about your dad's case because Gracie's afraid she'll lose a brother as well as her father."

"What if he sent you the messages? To scare you off, which would scare me off? For Gracie's sake."

"I wondered that at first," Elena said. "I mean, anything's possible. But Jake strikes me as someone who takes a more direct approach. And what about when we were followed to and from Bisbee? He was on duty that night."

"That's true. However, he might know about Marcus Rivera. He was a deputy during those years."

"I'll ask him."

Ridge had become a brick wall. Elena realized she wasn't going to get any further with him. Not today.

"Be careful, Ridge." She surprised them both by suddenly throwing her arms around his waist. "I couldn't bear it if you were hurt."

His hands settled on her shoulders. "Same here."

"Are you sure I can't convince you to let me keep helping?"

"Are *you* sure I can't convince you to stay in a hotel?"

"Maybe."

She pressed her face into his jacket as tears pricked her eyes. The feel of the rough material tickling her face felt nice. Too nice. His strong hands comforted her.

Wait. Weren't they just discussing the timing of things and

it being off? Yet, God had bought them together. He must, as Ridge had suggested, have a purpose in mind. If not to learn who was behind Pete Burnham's murder, maybe God meant for Elena and Ridge to explore dating.

Ridge was someone her parents would truly like. She could picture him and her dad talking sports. Imagine her mom insisting Ridge have seconds of her delicious cooking. And she was fond of Ridge's family, even Jake when he wasn't being overprotective and bossy.

Which reminded her, there was more to consider than her and Ridge when it came to their dating. She had to go into the station every workday.

"I'm not sure how Jake would feel about us. If we were to consider dating." Elena gazed into Ridge's ruggedly handsome features. "He is my immediate supervisor. Things could get awkward."

"Is there a policy against deputies fraternizing with in-laws of coworkers?"

"No, but—"

"Then don't worry about Jake. He acts tough, but he's not all bad."

"Says you."

Elena marveled a little at how easily they could discuss dating. It seemed they were no longer partners investigating crime. Now, perhaps they were potential romantic partners. How was it possible to feel bad and happy at the same time?

"I'd also hate for the chief to think I'm using you as a way to make points with my immediate supervisor," she added.

"The chief's smarter than that."

"It's something to think about before we…commit."

"No need to feel rushed, Elena."

She appreciated him recognizing and considering her concerns.

"I promised myself I wouldn't consider getting involved

with anyone until I finished renovating the ranch. I'm still a ways away."

"We start slow then," she said. "See how things go."

"Slow and steady."

That had a nice ring to it. Dating was complicated. And risky. And full of potential pitfalls. She, too, had made promises to herself that seeing Ridge romantically would break. Yet, somehow, he'd breached the barriers she'd carefully erected.

No, that wasn't true. If she were honest with herself, she'd admit she'd lowered those barriers in the first place—for him. She hadn't done that before. Hadn't allowed it. There must be a reason.

Ridge was different. What she felt for him was different. And he had feelings for her that he openly admitted. Could he be the right man for her?

"You free this weekend?" he asked. "We could go to a movie."

She smiled at the shift from their pretense of fake dating to this request for a real date. "I'd love to see a movie with you."

Ridge held her chin between his forefinger and thumb and dipped his head. She let her eyes drift close, waiting for his lips to find hers.

All at once, the sound of shattering glass split the air. Elena's eyes flew open, and she spun. "What was that?"

Ridge pushed her away. "Get out of here," he shouted.

She disobeyed and instead moved toward the sound. Her heart seized inside her chest at the sight of broken glass shards lying in a pile not fifteen feet away from where they stood. Flames erupted from a puddle of liquid and, within seconds, spread along the barn floor.

"Oh no!" She turned and grabbed Ridge by the arm, acrid smoke starting to fill her lungs. "We have to extinguish the fire. Do you have a water hose?"

"In front of the barn. I'll get it." He pushed her again. "You head to the house. Call 9-1-1."

She saw the reason for his urgency. The flames were already engulfing the bales of straw, consuming them with the ferocity and speed of an enraged beast. In another moment, the old wooden stalls would catch fire, and the barn would go up like a tinderbox.

Above the crackle of the fire, she heard a loud, panicked braying.

"Minnie Pearl!" Elena started running toward the little donkey's stall, the flames now precariously close.

"Elena, no! Come back."

A jagged arrow of fear cut through Ridge and launched him into motion. Someone had thrown what appeared to be a Molotov cocktail through the barn window. Whatever flammable liquid they'd used had instantly ignited and spread at an alarming speed.

She either hadn't heard him or refused to listen. Darting along a narrow space between the fire and the stalls, she headed straight toward Minnie Pearl.

"Wait!" He chased after her, his only thought of protecting her from harm.

In a matter of seconds, the fire had tripled in size. Ridge had never seen anything like it.

The stack of hay bales burned like a giant bonfire, the flames reaching ten feet high. Heat blasted him in the face. It must be worse for Elena who was closer.

Terror drove him ahead. At last, he reached her. "Elena!"

She didn't turn around, not even when he grabbed a fistful of her jacket and pulled. Flames closed in on all sides. The only avenue of escape was forward.

Releasing an anguished cry, she wrenched free of his grasp. "Elena!"

Somehow, she reached Minnie Pearl's stall unscathed. Sliding the latch, she threw open the door and tumbled in, Ridge on her heels. Minnie Pearl stood in the corner, her long ears pinned back, her eyes wide and glassy with fright. Rather than greet the two humans as her rescuers, the donkey cowered and shrank farther into the corner.

Outside the stall, the fire continued to grow. The air sizzled, searing Ridge's lungs. Smoke absorbed every molecule of oxygen, making breathing difficult. He considered shutting the door, but then they'd be trapped inside with no avenue of escape. Burning embers, glowing red as a hot poker, floated up and away, landing several feet away where they ignited new fires.

Please, Lord. I beg You. Guide us away from this inferno and lead us to a safe haven.

"Elena, if we don't get out now, we'll die."

"We have to save Minnie Pearl."

She locked her arms around the donkey's neck and attempted to pull her from the corner. Minnie Pearl was living up to the reputation of her species and refused to budge.

Ridge admired Elena for her bravery and her compassion. He was equally annoyed at her complete disregard for their well-being.

"She's not going anywhere," he said.

"And neither am I."

Good heavens, she was as stubborn as the donkey. He also thought he could fall in love with her, given half the chance.

The revelation was like a kick in the pants. "Hold on," he hollered and squeezed himself between Minnie Pearl and the wall. "Get ready," he told Elena.

She braced her legs.

Ridge planted his palms on Minnie Pearl's rounded rump and shoved with all his might.

Elena tugged. The diminutive donkey was remarkably strong and remained rooted in place. Resting wasn't an option. Ridge shoved again, encouraging Elena.

Minnie Pearl let out a strangled squeal and then lunged

forward. Once going, she didn't stop and rocketed out of the stall, knocking Elena to the ground.

Ridge rushed to her side and knelt. "Are you okay?"

"I'm fine."

"Can you walk?" He stood and yanked her to her feet, one eye on the nearby flames. "We need to get out of here."

She took a step and another, with more confidence. "What about Minnie Pearl?"

"She's long gone."

Holding her hand, Ridge approached the open stall door. The flames blocked their way, dancing high above their heads. He assessed their options. There was only one.

"Head left toward the back of the barn and out the door we went through that day I took you to the well house. Remember?"

"Yes."

"Cover your nose and mouth with your arm and duck your head." He squeezed her fingers. "Ready?"

She nodded.

Together, they rushed out of the stall and sprinted left through the flames. They were fast, and nothing caught fire. Even so, the intense heat struck them with a force that had Ridge remembering scary stories from Sunday school when he was a child. His eyes stung and watered. His vision blurred. His heart pounded.

Once they were past the flames, they hurried through the barn's rear door. Outside, they stopped running and coughed until their lungs cleared. Then they were on the move again.

"Call 9-1-1," Ridge shouted as they ran along the side of the barn to the front. "I'll get the hose."

At the hose bib, he flipped the spigot. Water flowed in a steady stream. He unfurled the hose and dragged it inside the barn. Using this thumb to create a spray, he aimed the water at the flames, moving his arm in a wide arc to cover a larger area.

Elena stood just outside the barn, her phone pressed to her ear. Did she never listen? He'd told her to go to the house.

While Ridge continued dousing the flames, she appeared beside him. "The fire department's on their way."

"Good." He inclined his head. As long as she refused to listen, she might as well be useful. "There's a fire extinguisher in the tack room."

She went to fetch it, returning a half minute later.

"Can you operate that?" he asked.

She pulled the pin and aimed the nozzle toward the fire. White foam sprayed out.

"Hit the flames from that side. Spray along the stall doors. I'll get this side."

Together, they succeeded in impeding the fire's progress. When the fire truck arrived five minutes later, the fire was a quarter contained.

"Stand back," the captain instructed Ridge and Elena.

They watched from the sidelines as, with their superior equipment, the fire crew extinguished the remaining blaze in a matter of minutes. When they were done, all that remained was a huge smoldering, blackened patch covering half the barn floor.

Ridge surveyed the damage. The scorched stall doors could be repaired or replaced. His new rubber mats were a lost cause, however. The generator and compressor were questionable. Water damage was extensive.

"You all right?" he asked Elena.

"Yeah." She wiped a black smudge from her forehead. "Minnie Pearl's standing by the house. She looks unharmed."

"Good. I figured she'd run to safety once she got away from the fire."

"What are you going to do with her? She can't stay in the barn."

"Put her in the round pen for a week until the barn airs out," he said. "She'll be fine with a bucket of water and another of grain, and that'll give me time to make the repairs."

"You need help?"

"You offering?"

"Maybe." She tendered a weak smile. They'd been through a lot the past hour, and her fortitude impressed him. "I'm sure there are members of Hillside Church who will volunteer the minute they hear what's happened."

"You can always count on your church family to step up in a time of crisis."

The fire captain joined them. "You're very fortunate," he said. His crew was giving the barn floor a thorough soaking to be on the safe side. "All in all, this could have been much worse."

"I agree." Ridge wiped his grimy hands with a handkerchief from his jeans pocket. "Very fortunate." *Thank You, Lord.* "Glad my insurance policy is paid up."

At that moment, two sheriff's SUVs arrived. Chief Dempsey climbed out of the first one and Jake the second. Elena hadn't needed convincing to call the chief this time. The fire was no small threat or scare tactic. Someone had tried to hurt, if not kill them and nearly succeeded.

Ridge would have nightmares for weeks, if not for the rest of his life. He could still see Elena running through the flames and feel his terror that her clothes would catch fire.

"Captain Gates." The chief acknowledged the fire captain.

"Chief Dempsey."

The two men shook hands and chatted briefly before the fire captain turned to Ridge. "We're almost done here. We'll leave as soon as we put our equipment away."

"Thanks again for your help."

"Glad you and the deputy are all right and the damage wasn't worse." He walked off to rejoin his crew.

Amen to that, thought Ridge.

Jake clasped his shoulder. His usually tough exterior had

given way to deep concern. Ridge rarely saw his brother-in-law unnerved.

"How you doing, pal?" Jake asked.

"Honestly? I've had better days."

"Man, this is awful." His brother-in-law's gaze explored the damage. "Gracie's worried about you."

"I'll call her in a little while."

"Elena, you hanging in here?" The chief scrutinized her. "You look pale."

"I'm fine." She nodded stoically. "The paramedic checked us over, said our oxygen levels were good. Real good, in fact."

"Heard you're pretty handy with a fire extinguisher."

"She rocks." Ridge smiled fondly at her and placed a hand on her shoulder.

His actions didn't go unnoticed by Jake. This time, however, he didn't appear annoyed or suspicious. Just relieved.

"She does," the chief agreed, then looked around. "Which window did the incendiary device come through?"

The four of them walked into the barn and across the sodden, blackened mess on the floor. The acrid smell irritated Ridge's nostrils and stung his throat. How long would it linger?

"Here." He pointed to the small, broken window next to the storage room. "Elena and I were standing by the generator."

Jake took pictures with his phone. Ridge would, too, later, for the insurance claim.

"Any closer," the chief observed, "and you might have gone up in flames instead of the straw bales."

"True."

"I wonder if the person who threw the bomb knew where you and Elena were standing." Jake studied the window. "I'm going outside to have a look."

"Did you see anything at all?" the chief asked after Jake left. "Anyone?"

"No." Ridge shook his head.

"Nothing, Chief," Elena concurred.

"What were you doing when the bomb came through the window?"

She tensed, not wanting her boss to know that she and Ridge had been about to kiss.

"We were talking," he said. "We had our backs to the window and didn't notice."

Had the person who'd tossed the Molotov cocktail at them known they were distracted? Had they been watching Ridge and Elena? It was possible.

"The person must have walked onto the ranch," Elena said. "We'd have heard a vehicle."

The chief wrote an entry in his notebook.

Jake returned, huffing slightly. "Can't see the entire barn through the window, but you three were visible. The person could have aimed right at Ridge and Elena if they'd wanted to. I'm guessing they were either in a rush and blindly tossed the bomb or didn't intend to kill you."

"Notice any footsteps?"

"The ground is covered with them. Along with tire tracks and coyote tracks."

"Elena and I ran past there during the fire," Ridge said. "I walk the barn perimeter at least once a day."

Jake wiped perspiration from his damp brow. "You'd need a team of experts to make sense of that many footprints. There's no way we'll get approval for that."

The chief stuffed his notebook and pencil in his jacket pocket. "Come on, Jake. Let's pay the neighbors a visit. It's dinnertime, so most people will be home. With any luck, one of them noticed an unfamiliar vehicle parked down the road or a stranger on foot traveling in the direction of the ranch."

"Call me if you learn anything important," Ridge said.

"I'll be in touch. I may have more questions when I write up my report. In the meantime, you be careful, Ridge." He turned his attention to Elena. "You take the night off."

"But Chief—"

"No arguments. I'll see you in my office tomorrow morning. Bright and early."

"Yes, sir." Elena met his eyes briefly. She looked as if she knew what the chief wanted to talk to her about.

Ridge thought he knew, too. And if he was right, Elena wouldn't like it.

NINE

Elena sat at Ridge's kitchen table, trying to eat the chili and cornbread Ridge had prepared and having to choke down every bite. The Molotov cocktail and resulting fire had frightened her more than she cared to admit. More than she'd allowed him to see. She'd been running on pure adrenaline for the last two hours and had yet to calm down.

She'd never been that close to such a large fire. At first, she'd been convinced the hose and extinguisher would be useless. The flames had spread at an incredible rate, faster than she and Ridge could douse them. They might as well have been fanning the fire with pure oxygen rather than dousing it with water and retardant chemicals.

Finally, though, God had answered her fervent prayers, for her and Ridge's efforts began to have an effect.

Poor Minnie Pearl. Elena's chest ached at the thought of that sweet, gentle creature coming to harm. Another prayer answered. The donkey now resided, temporarily, in the round pen. Ridge had even found an old pony-sized horse blanket for Minnie Pearl to wear so she wouldn't get too cold at night.

He'd scolded Elena after the chief and Jake had left for rushing into the fire to save the donkey. She'd insisted she would do it ten times over, if necessary. He hadn't argued that point. And she'd understood he wasn't mad at her, but rather scared for her.

"Can I get you seconds?" Ridge asked.

How he'd managed to eat a giant bowl of chili and two generous portions of butter-slathered cornbread amazed her. Perhaps, for him, adrenaline increased his appetite rather than diminished it.

"No, thanks. It was delicious, though. You're right, you're a decent cook."

He smiled. "I did mean what I told the chief earlier. You rock, Elena."

She attempted a feeble smile. "I don't feel that way now."

"Most people would have panicked. Bolted or froze. You keep your head under pressure. Except for when you ran into the fire."

"If not for my training, I might have bolted or froze, too."

"I was impressed."

She let her gaze wander the kitchen, noting small details. She hadn't been inside Ridge's house since the day he'd found the gun and the strongbox. Since then, the new cupboards and cabinets had been installed, along with new appliances. "The remodeling came out great."

"Thanks. I'm happy with the results."

"Bathrooms next? Are you getting water-saving fixtures?"

He set down his spoon, propped his forearms on the table and studied her. "I think we can skip the rest of the small talk."

She'd been anticipating a more serious discussion and was surprised he'd waited until the end of their meal. "I've been thinking of ways to find out who threw the Molotov cocktail. The captain mentioned a fire investigation to determine what accelerant was used. Once that's—"

Ridge cut her short, his tone grave. "I want to talk about what happened today with us. Not a fire investigation and what accelerant was used."

A flurry of pinpricks raced along Elena's spine. She hid her anxiety by schooling her features into a neutral mask.

"Okay. I'm listening."

"You could have been hurt or killed today. That was the intention of whoever threw the Molotov cocktail."

"I disagree. You heard Jake when he checked the barn window. The bomber could have hit us if they'd chosen. Instead, they aimed a distance away. It was a scare tactic, Ridge."

"And I'm plenty scared. Had things gone differently, we'd be having this conversation in a hospital room—or worse, not at all."

"We're fine now. I'm fine." She stopped herself from reaching across the table for his hand to reassure him, convinced he didn't want or need that. He had a different reason for this conversation.

"I don't want your help anymore with my dad's homicide," he said.

Oh. They were back to this again. "Even discreetly?"

"It's too dangerous, and I won't be responsible for something bad happening to you."

She sat still, organizing her thoughts before speaking. "I get where you're coming from."

"Good. We're in agreement."

"But you won't make any headway on your own."

"I don't have to. After today and the fire, I'll have the sheriff's department behind me. They can't continue to ignore me. I'm going to talk to the chief about Marcus Rivera and the old photograph. And I'll tell him what we learned from Olivia Gifford. When the test results come back on the gun and the money, I'll have enough to go to the Bisbee police and demand they reinvestigate. Like they mean it this time. If they refuse, I'll go higher. The mayor's office. The newspaper. TV stations. Whatever I have to do."

Jake hadn't been joking when he told Elena that Ridge could make problems.

"What if the test results come back inconclusive?"

"I'll still have enough to apply pressure."

"I can help. I know the ins and outs of the sheriff's department. Their inner workings. I have friends like Trudy and my cousin who can come in handy."

Ridge shook his head. "Absolutely not. Someone wants us stopped. So far, they've settled for warnings. Next time could be different. But if the Bisbee police are investigating Dad's homicide, that will change the game. Whoever's after us won't dare endanger the detective currently on my dad's case."

"They will, Ridge. They did before. If not with gun and bullets, then money. We don't have proof, but according to Olivia, the former police chief was likely taking bribes, along with the mayor. Whoever is behind this has power and influence and they aren't easily intimidated."

"All the more reason for you to stay out of it. I won't meet your family for the first time at your funeral."

Her heart responded to the emotion flaring in his eyes. His words were coming from a place of caring, greater than any of her previous suitors had shown.

She suddenly wanted to stay safe. For Ridge and for their potential future.

Yet, she couldn't simply walk away from a grave injustice. It wasn't in her. "I can handle myself. You said so yourself, I keep my head under pressure."

"No. I've made up my mind."

He had, and she could see there was no changing it. Not today.

"Like I said before, Elena, this isn't your battle to fight." His voice had lost its harsh edge. "It's mine."

"I thought it might be ours."

"That's…that's not possible." He squared his shoulders as if steeling himself for something he didn't want to do. "I was wrong to have accepted your offer to help me at the start."

She winced at a sharp pain in the vicinity of her heart. Until now, she hadn't seen his decision to exclude her as a rejection, but it was. She'd been wrong all along, and his feelings for her weren't as strong as she'd believed. Neither were they as strong as her feelings for him.

"I appreciate everything you've done," he said, seeming oblivious of her internal struggle. "But I'm moving forward alone from this point on. The chief and Oscar are untrustworthy, until proven differently, and you work with them. They have eyes on you. One of them has to be the individual tracking your computer activity at work. Or the station secretary. We haven't talked about her much, but she's in the perfect position to monitor your every move."

Elena couldn't bring herself to let go. She was stubborn, yes. More than that, fear prompted her to action. There were two types of people: those who avoided danger and those who faced it head-on. She was the latter. She took matters into her own hands and would never be a helpless victim.

"You're right," she said. "We haven't considered Sage, which is why you need me. I can monitor her just as easily as she can me. And no one will be the wiser. At the very least, I can be your sounding board. I'm good at giving advice."

"Someone will see us together and become suspicious."

"No, they won't. We're dating. Couples who date spend time together."

Ridge hesitated, his expression changing. "We have to stop seeing each other."

Elena had anticipated resistance, but not this…this complete dismissal. One bump in the road and he called it quits? The sharp pain of rejection from earlier returned. Well, that was what she got for lowering her defenses, opening her heart and letting Ridge in. A man who wouldn't stick with her through thick and thin.

"I think you must have set a record," she said, her hurt taking the form of anger. "Two whole hours after we agreed to try dating, you kick me to the curb."

"It's not like that, Elena."

"No? Then what's it like? You were the one who insisted we test the waters, not me. I wasn't sure."

Contrition filled his features. "I'm sorry. I should have said we need to stop seeing each other for now. Once this has blown over, we can go back to the way things were before."

"That's worse, Ridge." Her throat closed, making her voice choppy. "I'm not something you can put down and pick up whenever the mood strikes."

"I'm not saying this well." He rubbed his forehead and started again. "Elena. You're amazing. Incredible. Smart and brave and capable. You're close to your family, have a strong faith, love your job, and you're trying to make a difference in the world. You're exactly the kind of woman I've been looking for and never thought I'd find." His dark eyes begged her to put her hurt aside and listen. "I'm trying to protect you, not cause you pain and certainly not diminish what we have. If I've done either, I regret it."

She let his declaration sink in and soothe the wounds his earlier words had inflicted.

"I'm not a delicate flower," she said. "I'm capable of protecting myself." She stopped him with a raised hand when he opened his mouth to speak. "But I do appreciate you not wanting to put others in jeopardy. That's admirable, and I respect you for it. As much as I want to join you on your journey to find the truth about your dad's death, I will abide by your wishes and back off. That's your call, Ridge."

His shoulders relaxed in relief. "When you ran into the fire today, I was terrified. I couldn't think. Couldn't function. Couldn't make my legs run fast enough. I never want to experience that again. And I can't be the one who puts you in danger's path."

"I didn't mean to scare you. Minnie Pearl… I was worried. The fire. It was headed straight for her."

"I know. I wouldn't have wanted to see her suffer. But it was hard watching you."

Elena nodded, still struggling to process her feelings. So much had transpired in the last two days. First, there had been the threatening direct message. Her stressful conversation with her dad and her family seeking safety in a hotel. Then, the kiss she'd shared with Ridge, their mutual wish to date. Next, the fire. Now this, Ridge wanting to take a break when they'd barely started. She was entitled to feel uncertainty and confusion.

"I'm going home." She rose, desperate for solitude and an opportunity to reflect. "But let me help you clean the kitchen first."

"Elena." Ridge also stood. "I don't want you to leave like this."

His statement hit her wrong. He'd squashed all her romantic hopes for them, and then didn't want her to "leave like this," as if she was the one at fault.

"What other way is there?" She glanced around for her jacket, forgetting she'd left it draped on the recliner by the back door. "We're not working together on your dad's case. We're not dating. We're not even friends."

"We can be."

"No, we can't." Since he clearly didn't want her help with the investigation, or even with cleaning up after their meal, she headed toward the back door. "And you know that, even if you won't admit it."

"Elena."

"You can't deal me a huge blow and then expect me to be fine."

"You're right. That was…insensitive of me."

"You want space, you got it."

Seeing him at church and around town would be difficult enough. She wouldn't make it harder by pretending they were friends or holding out for a future with him that would never happen. Let the gossipers talk when they saw her and Ridge keeping their distance and noticed their cool demeanor when in each other's company. Elena couldn't care less.

Tears filled her eyes. She had to get out of here. Ridge could not, would not, see her fall apart. The reason didn't matter. Pride or embarrassment or fury. She simply knew that him witnessing her vulnerability was more than she could endure today. Tomorrow, when she'd come to terms and composed herself, would be different. Then she could talk to him.

Ridge accompanied her outside. She stood on the porch a moment, ruthlessly thrusting her arms into the sleeves of her jacket.

"I'm going to follow you home," Ridge said, donning his own jacket.

"That's not necessary."

"It is."

He was doing it for himself more than her. She supposed she could let him. Besides, what would denying him achieve? Certainly not any satisfaction. Not for her, anyway.

Ridge walked her to her car. Of course he did. She opened the door, unable to look at him.

"Take care, Ridge."

He didn't let her escape and pulled her into his embrace. She pressed her palms to his chest, intent on pushing him away. Only she didn't. Instead, she buried her face in his jacket.

"I wish I hadn't been the one to come out here the day you found the gun and strongbox," she whispered.

"Is that really true? Because I don't wish that."

She shook her head and sniffed.

"God has a plan for us, Elena. I'm sure of it. We have to be patient. We'll be together when the time is right. I've waited this long to find you. I can wait a little longer."

Elena recalled Psalm 5:3. *My voice shalt thou hear in the morning, O Lord; in the morning will I direct my prayer unto thee, and will look up.*

"What if you never find out what happened to your dad and who's responsible?" How long would he expect her to wait?

"Can we cross that bridge when we come to it?"

She didn't answer. His ambiguous answer disappointed her, and she retreated.

"Goodbye, Ridge. Follow me if you want, or not. Your choice. Makes no difference to me."

She got into her car then, not waiting for him to answer.

The tears didn't come. Elena refused to let them. She was made of sterner stuff, she told herself as she drove home, all the while checking the rearview mirror and seeing the headlights of Ridge's truck.

Nothing had changed. She was in the same place she'd been a few weeks ago. A deputy sheriff with a promising career. A loving, close family. A nice, if small, apartment. A church home. A bright future.

Except now she felt an emptiness inside her. A giant hole with a cold draft blowing through. How could losing something she'd never quite had leave her with such a gaping wound?

Minnie Pearl stopped in front of the barn door and stared as if assessing the damage from the fire. Ridge came up to stand beside her and placed a hand on her withers. He'd been letting the donkey roam the grounds for a little exercise. She'd already attached herself to him and the ranch and wasn't the least inclined to wander. She followed him around like a puppy as he shoveled debris into a wheelbarrow and hauled it to the dumpster.

Opening her mouth wide, she let out an enormous bray.

Ridge gave her head a scratch. "I couldn't agree more. It's a mess."

Along with the rest of his life.

He'd spent the night punching his pillow and getting almost no sleep. As a result, he was downing coffee this morning like it was water and regretting almost everything he'd said to Elena the previous day.

Ridge was hardly an expert in relationships, especially when it came to breakups. He hadn't had enough practice, not with women he'd truly cared about. A professional rodeo competitor spent more than half their life on the road. That strained any relationship. A guy could only miss so many birthdays and holidays and dinner dates before a gal grew tired and gave him his walking papers.

Had his chosen career been all that dissimilar to his dad's drinking? They were both gone much of the time. How had he not seen that before?

His relationship with Elena had been different, however. He wasn't rodeoing anymore. He'd returned to Ironwood Creek with the purpose of settling down. Trying to find out who'd murdered his dad might have put off some women, but Elena understood and supported him. More than that, she'd been willing to help him. Too willing, to the point she'd wound up in danger.

All night long he'd asked God why. One moment, Ridge had been holding Elena in his arms, imagining their future together and all the amazing possibilities. The next moment, a bomb had exploded, and they were battling a fire. Then, he was telling her they couldn't see each other anymore.

He'd been intent on protecting her, refusing to be the one responsible for her coming to harm and drowning in guilt that she almost had.

But that was about him and his feelings. What he should have done instead was consider *her* feelings. Ask *her* what *she* was going through and how he could help her. Respected *her* wants and wishes.

Ultimately, he and Elena would have ended up in the same place—parting ways. There was no doubt in his mind, the danger had been too great. But the decision would have been mutual, not just his, and she'd have landed gently rather than like a fall from a three-story window.

Minnie Pearl brayed again. Ridge swore there was a harsh reprimand in the loud reverberations.

"I know, girl. I'd take it back if I could. Do you think Elena will answer the phone if I call?"

Minnie Pearl meandered off toward the house.

"You're probably right. Guess I should give her a few days."

The donkey kept going, her stubby tail swishing. She found a patch of early-blooming wildflowers beneath the ironwood trees along the driveway. Like goats, donkeys would eat most anything that sprang from the earth, as long as it wasn't poisonous.

Ridge headed into the barn where the tools hung. They had escaped damage from the fire. Yet, only a few feet away, the severely scorched storage room door would need replacing.

He traded the shovel he'd been using for a rake. As he lifted the tool off its hook, the gravity of the last twenty-four hours hit him like a one-two punch. His strength left him in a rush, and his knees weakened. Leaning his back against the wall, he closed his eyes.

"Dear Lord. Please watch out for Elena. Take her into Your care and safeguard her from danger. She may not think she needs protection, but she does, but she needs Yours. Help heal the hurt I caused her and let her be receptive to an apology from me. I know I've ruined any potential future with her, and that's on me. But I hope she and I can at least reach a point where she can stand to be in the same room with me." Ridge tried to chuckle, but the mirth wouldn't come. "If I'm not meant to learn the answers about what happened to my dad, give me the ability to accept that as Your purpose for me. But if I am supposed to learn them, please guide me on my quest. Thank You, Lord, for Your unfailing love. Amen."

The prayer restored him. He walked over to the barn aisle and began raking with a vengeance, mingling the ash and soot in with the dirt. A glance across the yard assured him that Minnie Pearl was happily munching on flowers. He might have to do something about that. He liked the flowers. They added to the ranch's hominess.

Just as he was working up a sweat—and working off his frustrations about him and Elena—his phone rang with his mother's favorite Blake Shelton song. He stopped and leaned on the upright rake. Gracie must have told their mother about the Molotov cocktail and fire. His sister had spent thirty minutes on the phone with him last evening, alternating between crying and insisting he quit being so stupid and abandon this foolish notion of his to get justice for their dad.

He put the phone to his ear. "Hi, Mom. How are you doing?"

"Ridge. Honey. Why didn't you call me? I had to hear about what happened from Gracie."

"Sorry, Mom. I was going to call tonight. I haven't had a free minute, with the sheriff's department yesterday and then with the insurance company and filing a claim this morning. Had to take a bunch of pictures and email them off. I'm in the barn now cleaning. There's a ton of repairs. I'm going to be busy for a while."

He had no doubt she'd called to pressure him again about selling the ranch. Here was the perfect reason, in her opinion. Someone had nearly killed him. He'd be better off getting away from the ranch and out of Ironwood Creek altogether. Drawing in a breath, he readied himself for the confrontation.

"I'm so glad you're all right." Tears thickened her voice. "And the young woman who was with you. The deputy sheriff. Gracie told me about her. Said she's a nice person and was helping you with your dad's case."

"Yeah, she is nice. But she's not helping me anymore."

"Oh?"

If Ridge admitted he sent Elena away because of the danger, his mom would use that to apply more pressure to sell the ranch.

"It was for the best," he said. "I didn't feel right involving her."

Not a lie, not really.

"I hope after what happened, you're giving up. Gracie said whoever was behind the bomb is sending you a warning. You have to listen, Ridge." Her voice cracked at the end.

"His murderer needs to be brought to justice."

"Do they? I know you're tired of hearing me go on about your dad, but even if you were to discover who killed him, would your life change?"

"I'd find some peace."

"Peace comes in many forms. One thing your dad wouldn't want is for you to miss out on what makes you happy because you're obsessed with a vow you made to yourself when you were a boy."

How did she know about that?

His mom and sister both accused him of being emotionally stuck. Were they right? And if he let go, what then?

Elena's face appeared before him, and he heard again his mom's words: "What makes you happy."

"I say this because I love you," she said with unaccustomed tenderness. "We haven't always gotten along, and I wish that were different. Before you say anything, I take full responsibility. I allowed my anger at your dad to bleed into every part of my life, including my relationship with you. That was wrong, and I'm sorry, honey."

Ridge needed a moment before answering. "I never expected to hear you say that, Mom."

She sobbed quietly before collecting herself. "I should have. I fell into a horrible habit I couldn't break. When Gracie told me about the bomb and the fire…all I could think of was that I had every chance in the world to be a better mother to you and never took it. You deserved more. You lost the father you loved. And you lost your mother, too, because I was driving you away. I realize it's a lot to ask, but…can you forgive me?"

"Mom…"

"Think about it. You don't have to answer me today."

Ridge dragged in a breath, the concrete block in his chest shifting to make room for something he hadn't felt in a long time: optimism for an affectionate and supportive relationship with his mom. He hadn't realized how desperately he craved that until this moment and how grateful he was for the prospect.

God had given him an opportunity to heal at least one part of himself. It was a blessing. He'd be a fool to reject it.

"When I was younger, after Dad died, I was a real jerk. I admit it. In a constant state of anger. Moody. Withdrawn. Raising me couldn't have been easy."

"You turned out great, in spite of me."

"In spite of *me* and because of *you*, Mom. And that's why there's nothing to forgive."

She sniffed. "You're my favorite son."

He laughed. "I'm your only son."

"That, too." Her smile reached across their connection. "I'd love to see you soon. Maybe I'll come for a visit. I miss the girls and Gracie."

"You can stay here, if you'd like. Ben, too," Ridge said. "I have plenty of room if you want to bring him along."

"I'll ask him. Thanks, honey."

He waited for her to mention selling the ranch. She had a surprise in store for him, however.

"I can check out the new kitchen. Gracie says it's gorgeous."

"Okay. Not the response I was expecting."

"Look, honey. I won't lie to you and tell you I think you should keep the ranch. But if Gracie's all right with your decision, then so am I."

"I'm hoping to buy her out soon."

"She mentioned that."

"Start buying her out, I should say, if she's willing to take payments."

"I'm glad for you, Ridge. Perhaps I've been wrong all these years and the best way for you to move forward is remodeling the ranch and raising cattle like your grandfather. Not selling it."

Moving forward. Restoring the ranch. Raising cattle. Giving up his boyhood vow to find his dad's murderer.

If he did all that, maybe he and Elena could start fresh. The idea appealed to him. If she was willing. That remained to be seen.

Dear Lord. What do I do? Please show me the path. Do I continue searching for the answers I seek and the peace I crave, or abandon it all and choose a new path?

Ridge needed to ruminate for a while. Search his heart and converse with God. And, it seemed, he had a visit from his mom to prepare for, one he was looking forward to.

"Mom, I need to finish up here in the barn and then head to the hardware store."

"Of course. I…just… It's…"

"What?"

"Nothing," she said airily. "I'll tell you when I see you."

"Tell me now."

"It's, um, about the strongbox of cash you found."

Ridge forgot all about his chores and errands. "What about them?"

"If you're not sitting down, you should."

TEN

Ridge didn't consider himself a wimp. He didn't fall apart when receiving bad or shocking news. His mom knew that about him. If she thought he needed to be seated when he heard what she had to say, there must be a good reason. She was about to turn his world on its side.

He made his way to the metal chair where he drew in several calming breaths before sitting.

"Go on," he told his mom.

She paused. "I... I'm almost certain your dad is the one who buried the strongbox beneath the well house. And that the money inside it was payment from the cartel for letting them transport drugs across the back side of the ranch."

Ridge had recently concluded as much and disliked what it implied—that his dad had been as much a criminal as the people who'd been paying him off. But to hear his mom all but confirm it...

His heart sank. His dad really had been nothing like the man he remembered.

"Why didn't you ever tell me?"

"I'm sorry, honey. Please don't be mad. I was sure you'd take what I said and go on a rampage."

"I might have. I still might."

"And invite another attempt on your life? You're smarter than that. And you don't want the deputy sheriff to get hurt."

His mom had that right.

"Listening to you," she went on, "I'm confident you'll make the best decision, which is passing what I'm telling you on to the authorities and letting them do their job instead of you trying to do it."

Ridge was glad his mom had suggested he have a seat because he felt as if the ground beneath him were shifting.

"If that money came from Dad, why did he bury it rather than use it for the family and the ranch? Why didn't you insist on it if you knew he was taking a kickback? And more importantly, why didn't you dig up the money years ago?"

Her sigh said he was asking a lot of questions. "First of all, in the beginning, I wasn't entirely sure he was on the cartel's payroll. Of course, I had a strong suspicion. But whenever I asked, he denied it. In hindsight, I think he believed he was protecting us. You and me and your sister. The less we knew, the less danger we'd be in. And, frankly, part of me resisted knowing the truth. As long as I was ignorant, I could pretend all was well. Then one day, several weeks before he died, I overheard your dad talking on the phone with the auto repair shop about having my car repaired. It had been sitting in our garage for two months, not drivable."

"I remember," Ridge said.

"They wanted eight hundred dollars. If your dad had that kind of money, he wouldn't have spent it on repairing my car's transmission."

"Unless there was more where that came from."

"Right," his mom agreed. "After he mysteriously produced the money to repair my car, I couldn't pretend any longer. We argued all the time. No amount of money was worth the risk. There'd been one murder by then. Everyone knew the cartel was behind it, even though there was no proof. I was scared for all of us."

"I don't blame you, Mom."

"I decided then and there to find the money, if it could be

found, and leave town with you kids. Believe me when I say, I searched the house and barn from top to bottom. I never found anything, which made me all the more angry and fearful. I became convinced people were following me whenever I left the house."

"Were they?" Ridge couldn't imagine his mom's terror.

"Maybe. I think so. When your dad died, I searched again for the money and again found nothing. I'd decided either someone had scammed him out of it, he drank it away or his murderer stole it. I was so furious at him. For dying and for dying without giving me the money we desperately needed."

Ridge could see how his mom would come to those conclusions and how she could have carried a grudge against his dad, both while he was alive and after his death.

"There's something I don't understand. Why did he keep lying to you about the money? Obviously, your ignorance wasn't keeping you safe."

"Shame, is my guess," his mom said. "Not the taking of the money, that didn't bother your dad, but that he frittered it away instead of giving it to his wife and children who, at times, were living on the brink of poverty."

Ridge wondered if shame was what had driven his dad to take money from the cartel in the first place. Except forty thousand dollars seemed like an awful lot. And his dad cooperating with the cartel didn't explain the argument with the stranger in the barn and the accusations the man had made.

"Did Dad have any morals whatsoever?"

"Don't be so hard on him, son. He was hardly the only one on the take. There's no excuse for what he did, of course. But sometimes, when it comes down to providing food and clothes for loved ones or going hungry, the choice to look the other way is easy. Not to mention the cartel didn't accept no for an answer. They hurt people to get what they wanted."

"That's true." Ridge wouldn't have wanted to be in his dad's shoes.

"Unfortunately, for us, money burned a hole in your dad's pocket. I often ask myself, if he hadn't partnered with the cartel, would he have quit drinking and gotten his life together."

"He may not have had a choice," Ridge said.

"Things certainly ended badly for anyone who went against the cartel." His mom released a trembling sob.

"I don't remember any of this."

"I'm surprised. Your dad and I bickered constantly. I hated that he was more than likely aiding the drug trafficking. I hated worse that he drank up most of the money. Most of all, I hated that there was nothing I could do to change those circumstances. Not without putting myself and my children in danger."

Guilt squeezed Ridge's chest. As a boy, he'd tuned out his parents' arguments, believing they were about only his dad's drinking. If only he'd listened to their words, maybe he could have stopped his dad. "I'm sorry you went through all that."

"When I'd ask you not to stir up trouble by digging into your dad's death, it's because I saw what happened to people who crossed the cartel."

He saw that now. "I was wrong to cause you so much worry."

"It's not your fault. Your dad is responsible."

The last vestiges of the unrealistic image Ridge held of his late father evaporated into thin air. "He really was a terrible person."

"No, he wasn't," his mom insisted. "Please don't think that, honey. He was an alcoholic. He had a disease. I wish he'd tried harder to fight it because he had a beautiful spirit and an amazing capacity to love, which you know because he showed you that every day. For me, I should have been a better wife."

"You're not to blame."

"No one is. We were all victims and in a situation beyond our control."

"Were we? Couldn't we have moved?"

"It wasn't that simple. Your dad refused to sell the ranch his father had built from the ground up. He was determined it remain in the family. Then, after your dad was killed, the cartel had eyes on us. If I had said or done anything that put them or their operation at risk of discovery, they'd have me killed, too. By staying, allowing them to watch my every move, I protected you and Gracie."

"There's one thing I don't understand. If you knew how Dad really died, why did you always tell me you thought he'd been drunk and fallen?"

"Again, to protect you and Gracie. As long as you both were ignorant of the cartel, you remained safe. I escaped Ironwood Creek as soon as I could."

"After I left home to rodeo."

"Gracie was married to Jake, a deputy sheriff who knew about the cartel and would safeguard her with his life. You were on the road most of the time. Years had passed during which I'd shown the cartel I could be trusted. And then, Sheriff Cochrane was elected. Right from the start, he made it his mission to drive the cartel from Ironwood Creek with his crack-down-on-crime program. The town went from being the busiest drug route in the southwest to a quiet and safe community that attracted tourists."

Ridge rubbed his forehead, struggling to absorb all the information his mom had told him. This had to be the most incredible conversation of his entire life. Not only had he mended an eighteen-year-old rift between him and his mother, he'd learned astonishing details about his hometown and neighbors and parents. It was as if his mom were describing complete strangers.

He forced himself to refocus. Too many unanswered questions continued to plague him.

"Forty thousand dollars is a huge sum. Dad obviously didn't drink up all the money the cartel paid him. Do you think it's possible he stole it?"

His mom hesitated before responding. "I've considered the possibility. In a way, it makes sense."

"Except, not to malign Dad or anything, but he never struck me as being stealthy and the type to construct elaborate plans."

"He could have robbed one of the drug runners. Lain in wait for him along the route and pulled a gun on him."

Ridge envisioned his dad stepping in front of the drug runner's four-wheel-drive vehicle in the middle of the night and pulling a gun on the driver, his face covered by a mask. "That would have been incredibly dangerous, if not insane."

"And something your dad might have done."

"He might have." One thing didn't make sense to Ridge, however. "Except why would Dad have stolen money if he was being regularly paid by the cartel to let them use the ranch?"

Again, his mom's voice filled with sorrow. "You know how your dad was. A dreamer. Head in the clouds when it wasn't in the bottom of a whiskey bottle. He used to take you prospecting into those hills. Twice he invested small amounts of money in get-rich schemes that went nowhere. He had this idea of turning the ranch back into a cattle operation, which made no sense as he was the one who sold off all the cattle we had. I couldn't talk any sense into him. He was determined to buy some calves and repair the barn."

"He was?" Is that where Ridge had gotten the idea? Had he heard his dad talking about it to his mom and the seed had been planted? It was possible.

"If I'd suspected for even a second that he was planning to rob a drug runner," his mom said, "I'd have knocked him unconscious rather than let him go out." She started to sob. "I didn't think he was serious about the cattle."

"Who would?"

"I've spent years either dodging responsibility or letting myself drown in it. Ben couldn't be more supportive and understanding. I don't know what I'd do without him. That's not to say I didn't once love your dad," she added.

"I know that. I also know he didn't make loving him easy for you."

"I regret so many things."

"You and Dad were in an impossible situation. You had no choice but to work with the cartel. I'm amazed you kept it together as well as you did.

"I had you kids to think of and protect. Everything I did was for you."

With sudden clarity, Ridge realized what he'd perceived as his mom's bitterness, anger and misery from living with an alcoholic husband was, in fact, her fear, worry, frustration and resentment from their forced partnership with the cartel.

How could he have been so wrong all these years? Being young wasn't an excuse. He hadn't been twelve for a long time.

"I wish you had told me all this sooner," he said.

"I probably should have," she admitted, her tone despairing. "Your constant pressuring of the authorities about your dad could have put you all in danger—not just you but Gracie and her family, too."

Ridge felt the impact like a punch to the solar plexus. He'd been selfish and single-minded, never taking his sister and nieces and even Jake into consideration, especially after Elena received threats and the bomber had set the barn ablaze.

His mom was worried about not being a good mother? She had nothing on Ridge, who hadn't been a good son, brother, brother-in-law or uncle.

"Please, honey," his mom said. "I beg you. Walk away from all this. Nothing good will come of it."

He was starting to think she was right.

"Isn't Dempsey the chief now? I always liked him. And, once you've put this quest of yours behind you, ask that nice deputy sheriff out on a date, work on the ranch and do whatever puts a smile on your face."

Her advice had merit.

"Pray on it," she added. "You have such a strong relationship with God, I'm sure you'll reach the right decision."

Ridge closed his eyes, his thoughts continuing to race. "I have a lot to think about." And he would pray on it. "Thank you for telling me, Mom."

"If you want to talk again, call me. Or we could find some time alone when I visit."

"I'll probably have more questions."

"I'm always available."

"Before I let you go—" He paused. "Have you ever heard of Marcus Rivera?"

"Hmm." She went quiet while she pondered. "He had a business in town. Investments or something."

"Ever meet him?"

"No. Why?"

"Elena, the deputy sheriff, found an old photo of him with the former mayor at a fundraising dinner. We were wondering if he had a connection with the cartel."

"I wouldn't be surprised. The cartel had plants."

That got Ridge's attention. "What do you mean by plants?"

"People placed in positions that would benefit the cartel."

"Like spies?"

"Kind of. There were rumors about the former mayor," his mom said. "And others. A councilman, as I recall. And a banker."

Marcus Rivera, too, perhaps, a prominent local businessman who dealt with finances.

"One last question, Mom. Did Dad or anyone ever mention the Hawk?"

"I remember *you* telling the police detective about overhearing your dad and the stranger arguing, and the stranger mentioning the Hawk."

"But that's all?"

"Once when your dad and I were arguing, he mentioned

the Hawk. When I called him out on it, he got mad and told me I was mistaken."

"Did you inform Detective Darnelly?"

"No. Only because I didn't want to alert them about the money in case the cartel came after us." She hesitated. "I had the impression Hawk was a code name."

"For a plant?" Ridge asked.

"For the plane that met the drug traffickers at Rooster Butte. Do you remember Mr. Vasquez who owned the market? Once, I overheard him talking on the phone to someone about the Hawk and that it was landing at midnight. We all knew about the plane. It was just another of those things we didn't discuss."

Of course. The Hawk was the plane. All the pieces suddenly fell into place.

He needed to tell Elena.

"Mom, I have to run."

"Call me soon. I love you."

"I love you, too. Bye."

He didn't hurry off to the hardware store after disconnecting. The conversation with his mom had not only lifted a weight from him, it had provided clarity. He needed a moment to reflect.

His mom had forgiven his dad. That felt good to know, and it gave Ridge an optimism for the future he hadn't had before. Maybe it was possible for him to have a good marriage and not make the same mistakes his parents had.

With renewed determination, he dialed Elena's number, praying she'd pick up. As one ring followed another, he told himself she might be busy at work and unable to answer.

He was mentally composing the voice mail message he'd leave when the ringing abruptly stopped.

"Hello." Her neutral tone gave nothing away.

"Elena. Hi. Sorry if I'm interrupting you. It's important."

"What is it?" she asked, still neutral.

"I just got off the phone with my mom. She told me things

about my dad and the money and the cartel that she'd been keeping secret all these years. It gives some insight into my dad's case."

"Ridge." She spoke slowly and with a trace of weariness. "You said yesterday you didn't want me involved in your investigation."

"I'm not investigating anymore." It wasn't until the words were out that he realized he'd made his decision. "I'm going to pass this information on to law enforcement."

"Really?"

"The problem is, I'm not sure who to trust. I'd like to meet with you and tell you what my mom said. Get your input." He swallowed. "You once offered to be my sounding board, and I need one right now."

She didn't immediately answer, forcing him to wait.

At last, she said, "Okay. I'm off duty in an hour. I'll come to the ranch. I just need to stop at home first." And then she hung up on him.

Elena ended the call with Ridge and sat with her chin in her hand, replaying their conversation. He'd sounded anxious. Her first thought had been that he was concocting an excuse to meet with her and convince her to give their relationship a second chance—not that she would. But then she'd changed her mind. He'd learned something. Whether it would shed light on his dad's case or not remained to be seen.

Ridge had said he didn't know who to trust. She concurred, having her own doubts about the chief and Oscar and even Jake, for that matter. Not because Jake was out to get her. Rather she speculated he might have sabotaged her and Ridge's efforts in order to protect Ridge.

There was no way he was the one behind the Molotov cocktail. Someone close to Jake could be, however. Someone else besides the chief and Oscar. Was it Sage? Olivia Gifford?

Elena's head throbbed and her heart ached, ever since she and Ridge argued yesterday, and he'd sent her on her way.

What was wrong with her? She and Ridge hadn't really dated. A few meals, evading the mysterious vehicle trailing them to and from Bisbee, strategy sessions, digging into old records together, and escaping a treacherous fire. Those things didn't count as courting.

Kisses did, though. She and Ridge had grown close in a very short time. That must mean something.

Dear, sweet Lord. I did come to care for Ridge. Do care for him. Should I see him today or call him and cancel? Am I the means for him to find out who murdered his dad? The one who can help him? Will I be hurt again?

The station door opened, and Oscar burst in with his usual reporting-for-duty energy. He took one look at her and stopped in his tracks. "What happened to you? You're a mess." He grimaced. "And you smell."

Elena sat up and shook off her ruminations, which had been getting her nowhere. Her current disheveled state was the reason she'd told Ridge she needed to go home first before meeting with him. Despite having washed up as best she could in the station restroom and running a wet comb through her hair, her skin itched and dark splotches stained her uniform. She couldn't wait to shower and change clothes.

"I fell into the dumpster behind the Gas Up and Go," she admitted.

"Fell in or went dumpster diving?" Oscar chuckled at his joke, his mustache twitching.

She looked away.

From her desk on the other side of the room, Sage tsked and rolled her eyes. She'd been sympathetic when Elena returned to the station, offering to help her clean up and producing a package of wet wipes from her purse.

"Leave it to a rookie girl deputy." Oscar shook his head.

Elena paid him no heed. This was just another pathetic example of how her fellow deputies didn't respect her or treat her as an equal.

"The Gas Up and Go was robbed."

"No fooling?" Oscar sat at the empty desk across from her. "What happened?"

"A young man, twenty-two years old, pulled a knife on the clerk. Demanded all the cash in the register. The clerk handed it over, which was the smart thing to do. Better than being stabbed. A customer in the back ducked into the bathroom and called 9-1-1. Thank God the perp didn't notice her. I happened to be only a few blocks away when the call came in."

"And you found him in the dumpster?" Oscar snorted, clearly finding the situation hilarious.

Elena squared her shoulders. "Yes, I did."

"What? No way!"

"Don't you have work to do, Oscar?" Sage asked.

Elena appreciated the support, but she was capable of handling Oscar herself.

"He was already wasted," she said. "Obviously not thinking straight. He grabbed a bottle of beer from the cooler before running out of the market, only to stop behind the building to drink it. When he heard my siren, he hid in the dumpster. Figured I wouldn't look there."

"He was wrong," Chief Dempsey said. He stood in the doorway between his office and the main room. "Elena did all right. She got her man, and the Bisbee police collected him an hour ago and took him into custody. Guy had a half dozen priors there. He'll have a nice stay at the city jail until everything is sorted out and he goes before a judge."

"By falling into the dumpster and getting covered with... is that horse manure?" Oscar's amusement rang in his voice and shone in his eyes.

"Sawdust," Elena said. "They use it to clean up spills."

"Well, I hope whatever spills they cleaned up come out of

your uniform." The other deputy couldn't hold back any longer and erupted in laughter.

"That's enough." The chief's brusque tone quieted Oscar.

"I'm just having a little fun with her, Chief."

"Let's get to work. Elena, your shift's almost over. If you want to leave a little early, go ahead."

"I wouldn't mind. Thank you, Chief." She rose and went into the breakroom to collect her purse and personal items.

When she reentered the main room, the chief hailed her from his office. "You have a second before you leave?"

She made the mistake of glancing in Oscar's direction. He pinched his nose and squeezed his eyes shut as if being assaulted by a strong stench.

Ignoring him, she walked head held high into the chief's office. He sat at his desk, shuffling through a stack of papers. In her grimy state, she stood rather than soil a visitor chair.

"Yes, sir?"

He set the stack of papers aside. "Wanted to let you know, the results from the gun and strongbox are in."

"Oh?"

"Unfortunately, the lab director called while we were with the Bisbee police officers, handing over your perp. When I returned the call, the director wasn't available. No one else could help me. I'm waiting to hear back."

"Okay. Well, that's good."

"They found something, Elena."

"What?" She reached for the back of the visitor chair.

"The director didn't say what. Likely the information is too sensitive to leave on voice mail message."

Too sensitive. She wondered what that meant.

"Will you let me know the results as soon as you hear?" she asked.

"That's why I'm telling you."

"Thanks, Chief." She considered informing him that she was on her way to meet with Ridge, and he claimed to have new information on his dad. Her instincts cautioned her to remain quiet. Trust issues aside, the news was Ridge's to impart.

"See you tomorrow, Elena." He dismissed her with a nod.

"Stay safe," Sage called out as she passed by the secretary's desk.

Oscar was on the phone. From the conversation, it sounded as if he was about to head out. A Jeep had gotten stuck while attempting to cross Ironwood Creek. He didn't acknowledge her as she left.

On the walk to her car, Elena thought about seeing Ridge in an hour. She tried convincing herself that the knot of anticipation in her stomach was from the new information he had on his dad and had nothing to do with their personal situation.

Questions assaulted her all during the drive to her apartment. Should she tell Ridge about the lab results, or would Chief Dempsey? More urgently, did she even trust the chief? Granted, he'd told her about the lab director calling. But, in the larger scheme of things, that meant very little. He could be onto her and feeding her information to give her a false sense of security.

Her head ached worse than before. Ridge sending her away yesterday made no difference. She was still up to her neck in Pete Burnham's unsolved homicide.

ELEVEN

Ridge poured a scoop of pellets into Minnie Pearl's bucket and checked the bungee cord securing it to the round pen railing. Minnie Pearl liked to knock over her water and grain buckets, spilling the contents, which likely meant she was bored. He let her roam the ranch as much as possible, but she had to stay in the round pen for her own protection at night and when he was gone. Coyotes and mountain lions were known to attack small donkeys. Maybe next time he was at the feed store, he'd buy one of those equine enrichment toys she could bat around with her nose.

Finishing his chores, he made for the house, intending to wash up and change into a fresh shirt before Elena arrived. He was still grappling with everything his mom had told him about his dad, along with his eagerness at seeing Elena again. Common sense warned him to proceed with care. Nothing had changed overnight. She'd likely be reserved, if not hurt and angry.

He would only discuss his dad and avoid the subject of *them*. Now, if *she* raised the subject, he'd attempt to apologize for his poor behavior yesterday and to explain. But only if.

He entered the house through the back door, his glance darting right to the remodeled kitchen and then left to the new large screen TV dominating the great room. He'd believed the renovations and redecorating would erase the bad memories of his childhood and enable him to create positive ones. He'd been only partially right. The rooms were empty and too large. What was the point of a fancy new kitchen and new bathrooms and new furniture if he didn't enjoy them?

He'd have visitors soon—his mom and Ben were coming—and he wondered if that would make a difference. But Ridge wanted more than that. He'd refused to consider dating and falling in love for so long, waiting until he'd restored the ranch to its former glory. He was wrong about that, too. This house deserved to be a home, filled with a boisterous, joyous family.

Ridge deserved that, too. He'd denied himself the opportunity for happiness, afraid if things weren't perfect, his marriage would end up a train wreck just like that of his parents'. Except, look at his sister. She'd built a wonderful life for herself. Why couldn't Ridge trust himself to do the same?

"Lord," he said as he fastened the buttons on a clean shirt. "Once again, I'm asking for Your help. Which is the right path for me? I came home hoping to rebuild my life as well as restore the ranch. As if that would bring me the peace I desperately crave. Perhaps I'm looking in the wrong place. Is Elena the one for me? I think she could be. I'd like to find out. I ask You to provide a moment while she's here for me to tell her I'm sorry. If she isn't moved, then I'll—"

Ridge's prayer was interrupted by the ringing of his cell phone. He grabbed it off the dresser, experiencing a hitch in his breathing when he saw the name on the display.

Putting the phone to his ear, he said, "Afternoon, Chief."

"Ridge. Did I catch you at a bad time?"

"No. I'm waiting on..." He started to say Elena only to clamp his mouth shut. Revealing he and Elena were meeting might not be a good idea. "I have a few minutes to spare."

"Good. I wanted you to be my first call. I just got off the phone with the director of the lab in Tucson. The tests results are in on the gun and strongbox."

The bottom dropped out of Ridge's stomach. He stumbled his way to the bed and sat down on the edge of the mattress.

"The director went over the report with me," Chief Dempsey continued, "and emailed me a copy. It just hit my inbox."

"What does it say?"

"There was no usable DNA evidence on either the gun or strongbox. Both were in the ground too long."

Ridge let out a breath. "I was hoping for more."

"They were able to lift some fingerprints from the inside of the strongbox and from the plastic wrapping on the hundred-dollar bills. Before you ask, they found only your dad's."

This was consistent with what his mother had told him. His dad must have stolen the money from a drug runner and buried it. That part of what happened to his dad, at least, was solved. Just not who'd killed him.

"Well, Jake was right. That was a complete waste of time."

The chief cleared his throat. "Actually, that's not true. They did find something of interest."

Ridge straightened. "What?"

"There's a false bottom in the strongbox, which was discovered once all the stacks of money were removed."

"A false bottom!" He hadn't bothered to look beneath the stacks of money. There had been no reason. "Did it hold anything?"

"There are pictures attached to the report. I'll email you a copy."

"Just tell me."

"They found a gold chain. It fits the description of the one you gave the police eighteen years ago. The one you said you found in the barn after your dad and the unidentified man argued. They're running a DNA test, but that's going to take a week or two."

Ridge began to pace, his heart galloping. Here it was, proof he'd been telling the truth. Between what his mother had told him and this, the Bisbee police would have no choice but to restart the investigation.

"Thank you, Chief."

Without another word, he disconnected, his excitement diminishing as quickly as it had escalated. Should he have advised the chief to keep the test results under wraps? Which, on second thought, would be a waste of breath if the chief was in cahoots with the cartel or one of the plants his mom had mentioned.

He had to talk to Elena. She couldn't get here fast enough.

Elena closed the lid on her washing machine and pressed the start button. She'd opted to wash her soiled and smelly uniform separate from her other clothes and use double the laundry detergent. Even then, she worried the dirt and odor wouldn't come out. She may have no choice but to replace the uniform with a new one.

Oscar's reaction to her disheveled state annoyed her. Had she been a man, he might have poked fun at her, but in his next breath he would have congratulated her for successfully apprehending the thief and on a job well done.

Would she ever fit in and be accepted? It didn't seem likely, not in Ironwood Creek. Perhaps she'd been mistaken and hadn't found a home here after all. Her uncertainties grew when she recalled what happened yesterday with Ridge.

What an idiot she'd been. That was what she got for letting her guard down and developing feelings for him.

Had he been using her all along just to advance the investigation into his dad's murder?

No, he wasn't a duplicitous person. Not in the slightest. And how often had he tried to convince her to quit helping him, for her own safety, and she'd refused?

Still, her broken heart ached. He may not have intentionally used her, but she had let herself be useful to him. And that had clouded their breakup, if one could call it a breakup. More like an end to their friendship.

For a moment, she considered phoning Ridge and canceling their meeting. Whatever he had to tell her, he could surely accomplish on the phone.

Unless she *wanted* to see him again.

Elena squared her shoulders. Nothing could be further from the truth. She was done with Ridge Burnham. He'd rejected her. Elena possessed enough self-awareness to admit that. She wouldn't talk about it with anyone or admit her embarrassment, but she'd be honest with herself. Her beloved *abuela* had taught her that, along with many other important life lessons. The most meaningful lessons Elena had learned next to those she heard from the pulpit on Sundays.

With the washing machine running, she returned to the kitchen where she slipped into her favorite bulky sweater. Collecting her phone from the counter, she dropped it into the side pocket of her purse. Just then, her doorbell rang.

Elena's first thought as she walked across the living room was of her gun, locked securely away in the bedroom closet safe. Normally, answering the door didn't panic her. That was before she'd received threats and might have died in a fire if God wasn't watching out for her and Ridge.

"Don't be ridiculous," she mumbled under her breath. No one intending harm would come to her front door and ring the bell. They'd sneak around back and break in through her patio door.

She pressed her eye to the peephole before disengaging her deadbolt. Her taut nerves instantly relaxed at the sight of Jake. Nonetheless, she didn't immediately open the door. Why was he here, and what did he want?

"Hey, Elena." His muffled voice called to her through the door. "If you're in there, open up. I heard about what happened. Just wanted to check on you. Make sure you're all right."

She relented, disengaging the deadbolt and opening the door. "Hi, Jake."

"What?" He flashed a jovial grin. "You aren't gonna invite me in?"

"I'm on my way out, actually." She didn't mention her destination. He'd get the wrong idea, which he'd then pass on to Gracie. "And, as you can see, I'm just fine."

"I won't keep you long." His grin turned serious. "You've been through a lot, collaring that perp. Anyone would be shaken up."

Elena hesitated. It seemed he was here to extend an olive branch and was treating her like he might Oscar or any other deputy.

As she debated with herself, the door of her closest neighbor opened and a middle-aged woman emerged from her apartment wearing yoga pants and a sweatshirt. Her brows rose seeing Jake standing there, out of uniform. Did she assume Elena was entertaining a gentleman friend?

"Ma'am." He saluted the woman.

"Hello." She didn't bother disguising her avid curiosity.

"Afternoon, Beth," Elena said, forcing a casual tone.

"Um, see you later." After a few awkward seconds, the woman continued on her way, her gym bag slung over her shoulder.

"Come on in, Jake, but I've only got a minute." Elena spoke loud enough for her neighbor to hear. She wanted no misunderstanding. While nice, Beth very much liked to mind the other residents' business and talk about them behind their backs.

Inside Elena's apartment, Jake stood in the middle of her living room, his gaze roaming. "Nice place you have here."

"Thanks."

"Real homey." He nodded with approval. "Not what I expected."

She almost asked if he'd thought she used wooden crates and beanbag chairs for furniture.

"I appreciate you stopping by..." She glanced at her watch, hoping he'd get the hint and leave.

He cleared his throat. "Look, kid, I—"

"Kid?" Elena walked to the kitchen.

Jake followed her. "Sorry. Gracie's all the time nagging me about my inability to communicate well, as she says."

Elena leaned on the counter and waited for him to continue.

"You're a good deputy. I don't tell you that very often."

She didn't let her surprise show. "You don't tell me that ever. None of you do."

"We're a boys' club at Ironwood Creek. No denying that. We'll get better. We just need a little time."

She said nothing, thinking of Oscar's taunts an hour ago.

"We'd like that time, Elena. You'll see, things will improve." His features shone with sincerity. "Especially if you keep proving yourself like you did today."

Elena couldn't help smiling. They were boys, the whole lot of them. But maybe she, the only woman, could teach them and make them better at their jobs as much as they were supposed to teach her and make her better at her job.

"As far as apologies go," she said, "that wasn't the worst one I've heard."

"Good." He shrugged. "I'm also sorry about you and Ridge."

Elena stiffened. She'd told no one and didn't appreciate the personal remark. "I'm not sure what you mean."

"You and him. My mother-in-law called Gracie. She mentioned you and Ridge had a falling-out."

Elena almost asked Jake to repeat himself. Ridge had told his mom about the two of them? She hadn't realized he and his mom were close enough to share personal information. Not from what Ridge had said. And now it appeared Elena's name was on every Burnham family member's tongue.

Her stomach rolled. Here she'd been worried about her neighbor. This was much worse.

Jake reached out and patted her shoulder. "If there's anything you need, just give me a shout. I'm serious, Elena."

She couldn't bring herself to answer him. Jake might mean well, but he was her immediate supervisor and contemporary. They were law enforcement officers. She detested appearing weak or emotional in front of him.

Getting involved with Ridge had been a mistake for yet another reason. In hindsight, the last few weeks had been like a roller-coaster ride, filled with emotional highs and lows, excitement and fears, joy and pain, hope and disappointment. That was no excuse, however. She should have known better and stayed far, far away from him.

She hated missing church for any reason other than work, but maybe she should skip the next few weeks. Give her and Ridge some space. She could always attend the Wednesday morning bible study if she wasn't on duty. Except that would also give people like Jake and Gracie more reason to talk and possibly fuel the rumor fires.

Elena sighed. "Sorry, Jake. I'm running late for my appointment."

"Sure. I'll get out of your hair. Let me walk you to your car."

She turned and reached for her purse on the counter. "That's not necessary."

"It's getting dark. And someone threw a Molotov cocktail at you yesterday. You can't be too safe."

He said the last part from behind her.

Right behind her.

The hairs on the back of Elena's neck prickled. Her hand went to her side, seeking her gun that wasn't there. Every one of her senses urged her to run. Run now!

She ducked and moved to her right. Twenty-five feet away, the front door and safety beckoned.

Jake was quicker. He caught her arm in his vise-like grip and wrenched ruthlessly, nearly dislocating it from her shoulder and throwing her off-balance. She stifled a sharp yelp.

"Bad news, kid," he growled in her ear. "You're not going anywhere."

A knock sounded at her door.

Jake's meaty hand over her mouth muffled Elena's cry for help.

"Not a peep from you," he growled in a voice she'd never heard before. "You hear?"

She nodded, though she was tempted to bite his fingers. Better sense prevailed. The person standing at her door could be a cohort of Jake's. With everything that had happened to her and Ridge, the sergeant deputy couldn't have been working alone.

He abruptly thrust her into the counter. Hard. Before she could catch her breath, a blinding pain exploded in the back of her head. A shower of bright zigzagging lights erupted behind her eyelids. The floor rippled and rose up to crash into her an instant before her world went black.

Ridge tried Elena again. Four rings. Five rings. On the sixth ring, the call went to voice mail.

He disconnected and tossed his phone onto the kitchen table without leaving another message. Two were sufficient. A third wouldn't make her return his call any sooner.

Worry ate a hole in his gut. Elena wasn't one to play games. If she'd decided not to meet him, she'd have called or texted and not left him hanging. Same if she'd gotten held up at work, stuck in traffic or had car trouble.

Something was wrong. His instincts rarely led him astray, and right now, they were shouting at him.

"Where are you, Elena?" Anxiety coursed through him. In his next breath, he sent a prayer to God, asking Him to watch over her.

Pacing, he tried to calm himself with a dozen plausible reasons why she wasn't answering. Her phone was on mute. She was on her way and accidentally left her phone at home. Her carrier was experiencing a service problem and calls weren't going through. She'd dropped her phone, breaking it. Her battery had died. The list went on and on.

Ridge didn't relax. If anything, his anxiety escalated to the point he wanted to punch his fist through his newly painted kitchen wall.

He should have suggested she download the same locating app he and his family used, at least while they were investigating his dad's homicide. Why hadn't he?

When his phone rang, he dived for the table and grabbed it, his heart grinding to an agonizing stop when he saw the chief's name and number on the display. His fingers fumbled and refused to cooperate as he attempted to answer.

"Hello. Hello."

"Ridge? Are you all right? You sound out of breath."

"Is Elena with you?"

"No. She left the station a while ago. She said she was going home."

"She's not answering her phone."

"I know," the chief concurred. "I've been trying to reach her. I'd promised to call her with the lab results on the gun and strongbox. I thought maybe you might know where she is." Whatever suspicions the chief harbored about Ridge and Elena's personal relationship, his demeanor revealed no judgment.

"She's supposed to be on her way here." Ridge didn't explain why. "She's late."

"That's not like her."

"Neither is not answering her phone." Ridge resumed pacing. "Can you contact her phone carrier? Have them track her phone?"

"Not usually without a warrant."

"Can you get one?"

"That would take time," the chief explained.

Or was he intentionally stalling? Ridge wished he knew for certain.

"We don't even know that she's missing," the chief continued. "She's only been out of contact for an hour or two. There
could be a very rational explanation."

"If there was evidence of foul play, would you get that
warrant?"

The chief lowered his voice. "What are you planning,
Ridge?"

He was already shoving an arm into his jacket. "I'm on my
way to her place. I'll let you know what I find out when I get
there."

"You do that."

Ridge hung up. He may not trust the chief, but for now, he
had no other choice. Grabbing his keys, he remembered to
look up Elena's address in the church directory before bursting
through the door like a bull released from the bucking chute.

His truck tires showered dirt and pebbles into the air as he
sped away. He mentally calculated the time required to drive
from his place to Elena's and any available shortcuts. At every
stoplight and every delay, he pounded the steering wheel or
squeezed it until his fingers cramped. When her apartment
complex came into view, his concern waned. Finally, he was
here. Just as quickly, his worry returned when he drove past
her parked car beneath the metal canopy.

She was home. So, why wasn't she answering her phone?

*Please let her just be mad at me and ignoring my calls. I'll
take that any day over her being in trouble.*

Ridge pulled into a visitor parking space and jetted from
his truck. Evening had fallen by this time. It blanketed Elena's
complex in a blue-gray haze dotted by the lighted walkways,
exterior door lights and illuminated apartment windows. Except for Elena's. Her apartment was dark and eerily silent.

No, not entirely dark, Ridge noticed as he passed the living room window. A dim light was visible through a narrow
slit in the drapes.

He knocked on the door. When she didn't answer, he knocked

again. Pressing his ear to the door, he listened. No footsteps. No one calling, "Coming."

"Elena!" he hollered through the door and then pounded on it. Next, he tried the doorknob. Locked. "Elena, it's Ridge. Are you in there?"

A door opened. Not Elena's but rather her neighbor's. A middle-aged woman in workout clothes stepped outside. She paused, clutching a canister in her right hand, probably pepper spray or mace.

"Who are you?" she called, none too friendly.

"I'm Ridge Burnham. I'm a friend of Elena's. I'm worried about her. She was supposed to meet me and didn't show. Have you seen her?"

"About an hour ago." The woman stepped forward. "I was heading to the complex's gym. She was standing there at her door talking to a man."

A man? Ridge's alarm spiked. "Did you recognize him?"

"Never seen him before."

"What did he look like?"

"Just a guy. Thirty-five or forty. I'm not good at telling ages."

"What was he wearing? Did he have any facial hair or distinguishing features?"

"I don't recall any facial hair." The woman became flustered. "I… I think he was wearing a dark jacket and a ball cap."

Ridge fumed. She'd described anyone and everyone.

"I'm pretty sure she's gone," the woman said. "I forgot my key card to the gym at work. I came back here to see if I could borrow Elena's. When I knocked, no one answered."

"Did she leave alone or with the man?"

The woman shook her head, her disconcertment increasing. "I just said I left and when I came back, she wasn't here. I had no idea anything was wrong. The guy was smiling. She acted like she knew him. They weren't arguing or anything."

Ridge moved to the living room window, startling the neighbor who squealed and scooted backward. He pressed his face to the glass and peered through the slip in the drapes. Scanning the apartment's dim interior, he noted nothing out of the ordinary.

Where are you, Elena? What happened to you? God, please. Help me find her.

He saw it, then. A dark rectangular shape. Her purse! It sat on the kitchen counter. Elena wouldn't have left without it. Not willingly. And if her phone was in the purse, that would explain the unanswered calls.

Ignoring the neighbor, he dug his phone out of his pocket and dialed Chief Dempsey, who answered on the second ring.

"Chief. I'm at Elena's apartment. She's not here." He explained the details in a rush.

"I'm going to call the complex manager," the chief said. "Have them enter the apartment in case she's in there and unconscious."

Something about the situation and the man in the ball cap sat wrong with Ridge. He feared Elena was in serious trouble, and time was wasting.

"Chief, who else knows about the lab test results?"

"Our station secretary, of course. Oscar, maybe. He was here when I told Elena. He's out on a call now."

"Anybody else?"

"Detective Stewart with the Bisbee police."

The detective currently assigned to Ridge's dad's case. "What about Detective Darnelly?"

"Doubtful. He's retired."

"He could still have connections," Ridge countered.

"What are you getting at?"

"I'm just trying to figure out what happened to Elena."

"You wait there," the chief told him. "Let me get off the line and call the apartment manager. Once we establish whether or not Elena is inside, we'll determine our next step."

They disconnected. Ridge glanced around. The neighbor still stood near her door, watching him warily.

"Aren't there back entrances to these apartments?" he asked.

"Yes. We all have patios."

Ridge was about to go around to the rear of the building when he paused, still bothered by the man who'd visited Elena. "How tall was the guy talking to Elena?"

"Average. Not short. Not as tall as you."

"Thin? Fat?"

"Neither. Maybe a little stocky."

Detective Darnelly was every bit as tall as Ridge. It couldn't have been him. And Oscar sported a large mustache. The neighbor hadn't recalled any facial hair.

"What kind of ball cap was the guy wearing?"

The neighbor thought a moment. "Arizona Cardinals?"

Average height. A little stocky. Jake's favorite football team. The shock nearly felled Ridge.

He spun to face the neighbor. "The manager is on their way to check Elena's apartment. Can you stay and meet them?"

She nodded. "Okay."

He sprinted off, racing to his truck. If the manager found Elena, the chief would phone Ridge. And while he prayed that was the case, he didn't believe it.

Someone had Elena. That someone was either Jake or a partner in crime. Ridge just had to figure out where they'd taken Elena before something bad happened to her.

TWELVE

The instant Ridge started his truck, he dialed his sister. As he reversed out of the parking space, his Bluetooth kicked in.

Gracie answered with a bright "Hello there, brother."

In the background, the girls were chattering.

"Where's Jake?" Ridge asked without preamble.

"He's at church. There's a men's fellowship meeting."

"When's the last time you spoke with him?"

"Why? What's going on?"

"I need to know, Gracie. Have you talked to him since he left for the meeting?"

She hesitated. Covering the mouthpiece, he heard a muted "Girls, be quiet. Mommy's on the phone with Uncle Ridge. Go play in your room."

There was an indistinguishable verbal objection, but then the noise level diminished.

"He called me about an hour ago. Said the guys had a lot to discuss, and he might be home late." Gracie paused. "To be honest, he sounded a little off."

She had Ridge's full attention. He barely noticed the traffic as he sped out of town and toward the outskirts. "Off how?"

"Stressed. But not like work stressed. It's hard to explain. I didn't pay much attention, my mind was only half on the conversation. The girls have been testing my patience all day."

"I need you to be more specific, Gracie. It's important."

"What's wrong?"

Now it was Ridge's turn to pause. He debated whether he should level with his sister or continue to keep her in the dark.

"Elena's missing," he finally said. "It's possible, but not for certain, that Jake was the last person seen with her."

"Missing? Oh, my gosh. I hope she's all right."

"I need you to tell me everything Jake said to you."

"I already did. Well, other than he told me he loved me. But he says that all the time," she insisted.

Could Ridge be wrong suspecting his brother-in-law of foul play? He had no proof.

"Except…"

His sister's voice yanked him back to their conversation. "Except what?"

"He didn't just say he loved me. He said he's always loved me and the girls and that everything he did was for us. I thought he was talking about his job and volunteering so much at church. I told him I've always loved him, too." Gracie made a soft sound of distress. "You're scaring me, Ridge. Jake would never hurt Elena. He likes her. Besides, he's not that kind of person. He's good and thoughtful and caring."

Ridge had always thought so too, and he wanted to be wrong, if only for his sister's sake.

"Dial him and put us on a three-way call," Ridge instructed. "Let's find out where he is."

"Is that really necessary?" Gracie had become defensive.

Not unexpected. She loved her husband and was loyal to him.

"Please, Gracie. Just ask him if he's talked to Elena or seen her today."

"Fine."

A few seconds later, he heard ringing. She'd added Jake to their call. *Thank You, Lord.* Ridge waited, his jaw clenched.

Five rings later, Jake's voicemail greeting filled the line.

"That means nothing," Gracie said as the greeting played. "He could be busy."

"True."

After the beep, she left a message. "Hi, sweetie. Call me back when you have a second. Love ya. Bye." When she disconnected from Jake, she asked Ridge, "Happy?"

"Who else attends the meeting?" Jake asked.

"What?"

"Doesn't Mr. Harmon go? Call him."

"Ridge."

"I wouldn't ask if it wasn't important."

"Okay, okay."

She did as he requested, including Ridge on the call. They didn't talk for long. Once Mr. Harmon confirmed Jake never showed, they thanked him and said goodbye.

"There could be a very good explanation," Gracie said.

He hated hearing her insecurity, as he was sure she did, too. No one wanted to believe for one second the person they'd loved for years was capable of dastardly deeds.

"Have you checked the location app?"

"Hold on. I will." After a moment she said, "He's not appearing anymore." Her voice rose. "Ridge, what does that mean?"

"He may have disabled the app."

"Why?"

"I don't know." He wasn't about to admit what was going through his mind. "Call me the instant you hear from him." Ridge pressed his foot down on the gas pedal, accelerating.

"I will. And you call me when *you* hear from Elena."

"Will do." He phoned Chief Dempsey at the next intersection.

"Did Elena contact you yet?" the chief asked.

"No. What about the complex manager? Were they able to get into her apartment?"

"She wasn't there."

"I'm worried, Chief. I spoke to my sister. Jake never showed up at the church meeting he was supposed to attend. And my sister said he sounded a little off when they spoke earlier."

"What are you driving at?"

"I think Jake may have taken Elena."

"Jake? Are you nuts?"

"Have you heard from him recently?" Ridge asked.

"He's off duty."

"Would you try calling? See if he'll answer you?"

The sheriff grumbled but obliged. "Sage," he hollered. "Get ahold of Jake for me. Yes, now. Yeah, I know." An anxiety-filled minute of silence passed while they waited on the station secretary. "Okay, thanks." To Ridge, the chief said, "No answer. Which means nothing, Ridge. He could be out of range."

"Elena's neighbor described the man she saw at Elena's door. He fits Jake's description."

The chief cut him short. "Until I have a good reason to believe otherwise, I'm going to assume Jake's the fine and upstanding deputy and citizen he is and has always been."

Ridge wasn't deterred. "Is he driving his SUV? Can you locate him using the GPS device?"

"That's a stretch, don't you think?"

"What I think," Ridge answered, his jaw tight, "is that shortly after the lab contacts you with the news they found a gold chain in a false bottom of the strongbox, Elena mysteriously disappears without her purse and phone, my sister receives an odd phone call from Jake, who then goes off-grid, and a man matching his description was seen at Elena's door. All of that can't be a coincidence."

He turned onto the road that would take him to his ranch. He couldn't say why he was driving there, only that it was where his instincts were leading him.

The chief had yet to answer Ridge. Apparently, the man took a long time to consider. Or he had been in on the conspiracy behind Ridge's dad's murder from the beginning and was devising a plan on how to get away without attracting notice.

At last, the chief spoke. "All right. I'll see what I can find out."

Fortunately, no other vehicles were on the road when Ridge's truck momentarily swerved, the result of relief pouring through him. He immediately regained control and straightened the steering wheel.

"Thank you, Chief."

"I'll be in touch." The line went dead.

Ridge drove onto the ranch and parked behind the house. What should he do? Go inside, or maybe head to the barn? Waiting would be excruciating.

Stepping out of the cab, he heard Minnie Pearl braying from her temporary home in the round pen. He realized she must be hungry. Had he forgotten to feed her? Jogging toward the barn, he remembered he *had* fed her. Why the ruckus then?

She trotted back and forth across the pen, her large ears flopping. At the railing, she stopped and brayed again. Something had her riled. Coyotes? A rattler? A trespasser? Donkeys had excellent memories. Had the arsonist returned?

An investigation of the pen yielded nothing. But as he did his instincts, Ridge trusted Minnie Pearl.

Unable to keep still, he continued looking. In the barn, the remaining damage reminded him of the Molotov cocktail and fire. He sat in the metal chair and tried to read the lab report the chief had forwarded him on his phone, but he couldn't concentrate. Twice he started to call his sister, only to change his mind. She'd phone if she heard from Jake.

There was only one thing he could do. Letting his head fall into his hands, he prayed harder than he ever had before.

"Dear Lord. I beg You to keep Elena safe from harm. I shouldn't have put her at risk. Please don't let her pay for my mistakes. And if I've mistakenly believed Jake guilty of wrongdoing, I ask Your forgiveness and his. But if I'm right, and he's involved, please lead me to him so that I can save Elena. She's Your devoted servant, as am I. We need Your protection."

Before he could finish, his phone rang.

"Yeah, Chief. What have you heard?"

"I have a location for Jake's vehicle."

Ridge's chest seized. "Where?"

"I'll be at your place in five minutes. Meet me behind the house. Have your ATV gassed up and ready to go."

"The ATV? Why?"

"Tell me you remember the spot where your dad was killed."

"I do." He'd never forget.

"Good." With that, the chief disconnected.

Pain. It had taken the form of a pickax chipping away at the back of Elena's head. The tiniest movement on her part caused excruciating agony.

She moaned. Her mouth felt dry, and her jaw refused to work properly. Something big was lodged in her throat, and she couldn't swallow. Continued attempts caused her to panic. Forcing herself to relax, she inhaled through her nose until her racing heart slowed enough that she could focus.

Bit by bit, she became aware of her surroundings. A small stone dug into the right side of her face and something sharp— a stick?—jabbed her calf. Nearby, an owl hooted. Concentrating gave recognizable shapes to the inky forms surrounding her. Boulders. A bush. Cacti. She must be lying on the ground. But where?

A shiver ran through her. From shock? Pain? Fear? The cold? All of the above? The sweater she'd chosen earlier in her apartment provided inadequate protection now that night had fallen.

Her apartment. She'd been readying to meet Ridge at the ranch. And then… And then…there'd been a knock on her door. She fought to grab hold of the blurry memory floating on the fringes of her mind.

Jake.

She suddenly remembered a brilliant pain followed by blackness. He...he must have knocked her unconscious and kidnapped her. But why?

Because she and Ridge had gotten too close to the truth. And Jake was somehow involved.

Ignoring her agony, Elena tried to sit up—only to discover her hands were bound behind her back. A scream escaped, muffled by the rag shoved in her mouth and the gag holding it in place.

No! No, no, no! This couldn't be happening. Had Jake dumped her somewhere in the desert or mountains where no one would ever find her to die?

Her stomach clenched. She was going to be sick.

Elena fought against the nausea. If she vomited, she might aspirate and choke to death. Squeezing her eyes shut, she felt tears slide down her cheeks.

Dear Lord. I don't want to die like this. Not alone. Not without saying goodbye and I love you to my family or telling Ridge how I really feel about him. Help me find a way to save myself.

Sit up. She had to sit up and then stand. She tested her legs, ecstatic to find that her ankles weren't bound. Neither was she blindfolded. Once on her feet, she could get her bearings and walk for help. Wherever Jake had left her, there must be a road nearby. He wouldn't have carried her that far. He was strong, but dead weight was heavy and unwieldy.

Gritting her teeth, she ignored the dizziness and fiery jolts crisscrossing through her and tried to sit up.

"Here. Let me help you." Jake materialized above her. His voice held a combination of exaggerated mirth and cruelty.

She froze, terror invading her bones. She'd made a grievous error in judgment. Jake hadn't abandoned her. He'd been right beside her the entire time.

Without any warning, he grabbed her by the arm and jerked her upright.

Streaks of red and blue flashed in front of Elena's eyes.

She screamed into the rag as the invisible pickax split her head in two.

"On your feet." Jake unceremoniously hauled her up by the waist.

A wave of dizziness tried to knock her sideways. She had almost no time to steady herself when Jake leaned close and growled in her ear.

"Don't move."

She felt a sharp jab in her ribcage. His gun!

When he reached for her, she averted her head.

"I said, don't move."

Taking hold of the duct tape covering her mouth, he ripped it off in one swift move. Elena gave a yelp and then spat out the rag. Blessed air filled her lungs as she bent forward and succumbed to a coughing fit.

Jake chuckled. "Being a bit dramatic, aren't you?"

A moment later, her fit subsided. When she could finally talk, she croaked out a one-word question. "Why?"

"I think you know the answer to that. You and my brother-in-law are too nosy for your own good."

"Why are you doing the cartel's dirty work?"

"Ah." He shifted.

Elena began to panic again and fought her restraints. What was he doing? She tried to turn her head to see behind her. The jarring pain from her head injury stopped her.

She felt her hands jerk and heard a ripping sound. The next second, her arms fell to her sides like those of a rag doll. He'd cut the duct tape binding her wrists. Her hands tingled as blood flow resumed.

"Given the choice, I'd have left those and the gag. But my instructions are to make your death look like an accident, though I can't imagine we'll fool anyone. Duct tape leaves residue." He sighed with mock disappointment. "You'll just be another unsolved murder. Like Pete Burnham and the others."

Keep him talking, Elena told herself. *Buy time.* Ridge was expecting her at the ranch. When she didn't show, he'd attempt to reach her and then, God willing, go in search of her. Given the recent danger they'd been in, he'd be worried.

Please, Lord. Send Ridge. Let him find me.

Jake shoved the gun harder into her side. "Start walking."

She stumbled before gaining her balance. "Where are we going?"

"You'll see. It's not far."

They started climbing a rise, Elena in front and Jake behind her, his gun pressed against her back. They were in the hills, but where? Between her head injury and the darkness, she couldn't be sure of their location, but something about the area struck a chord with her. Glancing at the moon, she guessed it to be about seven or eight at night. She scanned the area for headlights. Those she saw were too far in the distance to notice her and Jake, much less come to her rescue. She was on her own.

"When did the cartel recruit you?" she asked. "After you first came to Ironwood Creek?"

"Oh, long before then. I was twenty and serving time for a burglary conviction."

"How did you get to be a deputy sheriff with a felony record?" She stepped carefully, not wanting to trip.

"Come on, Elena. You're smarter than that," Jake said. "The cartel gave me a new identity and sent me to police academy. I was their man on the inside from the very beginning." He sighed. "Ah, those were the good old days. Before Sheriff Cochrane was elected and forced us to…retreat. Now, we're just waiting for the next election."

"What happens then?"

"Cochrane won't win."

Jake's breathing became labored the higher they climbed. Elena's, too. They hadn't traveled far, but the grade was steep and the ground uneven.

"You can't know the outcome of the election," Elena said.

"But we can. Sadly, poor Sheriff Cochrane will become the subject of a very embarrassing scandal right before he announces his plan to run for another term. He'll not only decide to drop out of the race, he may even face some very serious charges."

"A real scandal or one your people fabricate?"

"Does it matter? The results will be the same. We'd have done it sooner, but the timing wasn't right. We didn't have our candidate in place."

Elena stubbed her toe on a rock and let out a low "Oomph" as she teetered.

Jake was less quick responding than before. Was he tiring? Could she use that to her advantage? He outweighed her by eighty pounds. But she was nimbler than him and in better shape. She could also outrun him, and the darkness provided cover. At least, she could under normal circumstances. When she hadn't been clobbered on the head.

One thing for sure, she couldn't outrun a bullet, and Jake was a good shot.

They reached the top of the hill. Elena saw the lights of Ironwood Creek in the distance. To her right, more lights dotted the landscape below, marking the location of houses and ranches.

"Keep moving," Jake barked. "A few more feet."

Elena obeyed, fear increasing with every step as coal-black emptiness appeared not five feet in front of her. Cold air rose from the depths to swirl about her and brought with it a message: she wasn't long for this world.

No, no! I'm not ready.

"We're here," Jake announced, huffing and puffing.

Elena started to tremble. Hugging herself did nothing to ease the violent quakes.

"Don't you recognize it?"

She stared as a fresh wave of terror consumed her. She

should have known where he was taking her, but her thoughts had been too fragmented to put in any kind of order.

"Come on, Elena." He pushed the gun into her back. "We're at the ledge. The same one I pushed Pete Burnham off."

Her voice quavered when she spoke. "You k-killed him?"

"I didn't want to. I liked him, actually. Pete was a friendly drunk. But I was under orders. He stole money from us. I gave him a chance to come clean. He lied. Claimed he'd give it back. But he didn't. He wasn't very bright."

"You were the man in the barn Ridge saw arguing with his dad."

"I was worried he'd recognize me when we first met. Apparently, the passing years dulled his memory. Plus, I'd cleaned up. A shave. A haircut. He wasn't looking for his dad's killer in the deputy sheriff dating his sister. It was a perfect cover."

Keep him talking. As long as I'm alive, I have a chance.

How far down to the ravine bottom? She tried to remember if she'd read that in the police report. If she jumped, would she survive? She was a dead woman if she continued to stand here.

"You'd have killed Pete even if he returned the money."

"That's true. Burnham sealed his fate the moment he robbed our man. The cartel doesn't tolerate disloyalty."

"The cartel being Marcus Rivera?"

"You are clever, aren't you?"

"Where is he now?"

"He left the country. He'll return after the election."

"The new sheriff may take the same zero tolerance stance on crime and the cartel as Sheriff Cochrane," Elena said.

"Our candidate will have a lot of money behind him. And money is what wins elections."

"Dirty money."

"You're taking this personal," Jake said, weariness in his voice. "It's business."

"Murder is business?"

"Murder is the cost of doing business. You'd come to learn

that if you'd been a deputy longer." He shoved the gun barrel into her back. "I'm tired of talking. I need you to turn sideways so it looks less like you were pushed and more like you fell."

An icy spike of fear pierced her heart. This couldn't be the end. She didn't want to die this way.

"I want to say goodbye to my family. Will you let me call them?"

"Oh, good grief. You aren't serious."

"What about Gracie? And your daughters? You're going to kill me and then return to them as if nothing happened? My neighbor saw you. Eventually, they'll figure out it was you."

She sensed a shift in him. "I'll miss Gracie and the girls."

"You're leaving?"

"No choice."

Elena swore she detected regret in his voice. "Why?"

"Marrying Gracie was a way for me to be accepted into the community."

"Except you fell in love with her. And you love your daughters, too."

"Shut up."

"What's going to happen to them after you're gone? No one will believe Gracie's innocent. She could go to jail. Your girls will be raised by someone else. Possibly a stranger."

"I said, shut up." He slapped her on the side of her head with the hand not holding the gun.

Elena cried out as her legs went out from under her. He hooked her by her sweater collar before she fell.

"Let me go, Jake," she said, whimpering. "Let me go, and I won't tell anyone. You can return to Gracie and the girls and your job, and everything will go back the way it was."

He laughed, a sharp, ugly sound. "If I let you go, I'm as good as dead. Rivera will see to that. I'm better off leaving. The cartel will take care of me. Give me another new identity and set me up in a new location. More importantly, they'll protect Gracie and the girls. If I *don't* do my job, their lives will be in danger."

"The cartel would kill a woman and children?"

"You don't understand. Theirs is a multi-billion-dollar business. Everyone is expendable. Including your boyfriend."

Tears blurred Elena's vision. "What will happen to him?"

"You two should have quit when I told you to. You were threatened. You were followed. But you didn't heed the warnings and kept sticking your noses in where they didn't belong. And now look. You're both going to pay with your lives. The next bomb won't miss Ridge by fifteen feet. It will land inches from him. Maybe while he's in bed, asleep."

Elena stifled a desperate sob. "He's Gracie's brother. The girls' uncle. If you care about her at all, you won't take him from her and your daughters. They'll need him after you've disappeared."

Jake didn't answer immediately. She thought, hoped, prayed she'd gotten through to him. That somewhere, deep down, he wasn't all bad.

"I've heard enough," he grumbled and knocked her in the shoulder. "Turn sideways. Let's get this over with."

"No, Jake. Please. Don't." Her bones dissolved to jelly. She reached out in a helpless gesture, only to drop her arms. Her life, her future, was slipping away. She believed with all her being that heaven waited for her, and she would gladly enter God's kingdom when it was her time.

Am I wrong, Lord, not to want to go yet?

She broke into sobs.

"Enough blubbering."

Jake pushed her the last few feet toward the ledge. Elena sensed the drop-off more than saw it. Shadowy shapes moved in the blackness below as if alive.

Would it hurt when she fell? Would her last earthly memories be of pain and fear?

"See you around, rookie."

Elena squeezed her eyes shut, every muscle in her body tensing in anticipation.

And then a sudden noise filled her ears, one that didn't belong there. One Jake hadn't expected to hear given his reaction.

"Son of a—"

He turned away from her, shoving into Elena as he did. She momentarily teetered on the edge of the precipice before regaining her balance at the last second. Her breath fast and ragged, she dared to look and saw what had angered her captor.

The unexpected sound belonged to an engine, and a pair of headlights coming up the rise straight toward them.

THIRTEEN

Every cell in Ridge's body had turned to red-hot fury at the sight of Elena standing at the ledge in the same spot his dad must have fallen and his brother-in-law, a man Ridge had once trusted, about to push her off.

She was alive. Jake hadn't succeeded.

Thank You, Lord, for leading us to her in time.

"Wait here," the chief said and climbed off the back of the ATV.

Wait? Was the man serious?

Brandishing his weapon, the chief approached Jake and Elena.

Ridge was right behind him, disobeying orders. "Elena, are you all right?"

She and Jake stood in the twin beams of the headlights. Fear distorted Elena's features. Anger, Jake's. In the harsh glow, he didn't resemble the man Ridge had known all these years.

A memory tugged. The barn. His dad and the stranger.

"Step away from her," the chief ordered, "and drop your gun."

Jake stared directly at Ridge, ignoring the chief. "You always were a smart one. That's why you did so well rodeoing. You had good sense when it came to assessing the bulls and your competition. And now, it seems, you figured me out."

Ridge saw it then. The resemblance to the stranger in the barn who'd argued with his dad hours before his death. How could he have missed it? If he'd noticed, they wouldn't be here now, and his sister wouldn't have married a cartel operative.

"I'm taking you in, Jake," the chief said.

"We'll see about that."

Jake spun and reached for Elena. She shrieked as he pulled her roughly against him, using her as a shield. His gun moved from her side to her head, and she froze, not daring to move.

Ridge didn't realize he'd taken a step forward until the chief growled, "Stay put, Ridge. Don't make things worse."

It required every ounce of his willpower to grind to a halt. "Elena," he called out, his voice choked. "Are you all right?"

She nodded shakily. She was anything but all right. A man with no regard for human life held her hostage.

"Be reasonable, Jake," the chief said with remarkable calm. "You won't get far."

"I don't have to." He sneered at the chief. "There's a pickup point less than two miles from here. The ATV should get us there no problem."

"Us?" Ridge demanded.

"Can't leave my insurance policy behind now, can I?" He lifted one shoulder in a casual shrug. "If you and the chief agree to cooperate, I'll leave the two of you here tied up. I'm pretty sure you have some rope in that storage case on the ATV. Someone will find you in a day or two."

Ridge's fists clenched at his sides. "What about Elena?"

"There's collateral damage in every negotiation."

A vile taste filled Ridge's mouth. How could he have treated Jake like family? Considered him a friend? Spoken highly of him? How could this monster hold his daughters in his lap, profess to love them, and all the while be plotting how to execute his next crime or kill his next victim?

"Leave her with us," Ridge said, his heart being ripped from his chest. He'd yet to tell Elena his true feelings for her or describe the bright, happy future they could have together. What if he never got the chance? "You don't need her."

"But I do," Jake insisted.

"This is your last chance, Jake," the chief reasoned. "If you let her go, there's a possibility things will go a little easier on you."

"Easier on me?" He laughed only to abruptly stop at the distant sound of an approaching siren. Anger morphed into the first signs of panic as reality sank in.

"You didn't think we came alone?" the chief asked. "Oh. You did. That's on you. All these years of us working together, you have to know I'm better at my job than that."

Just as Ridge wondered how he could have been fooled by Jake for all these years, he wondered why his instincts hadn't told him to trust Chief Dempsey.

Jake glanced around, his expression wild and his brow shining with sweat in the glow of the headlights. "This does change things." He craned his neck and peered over the ledge, all the while holding the gun to Elena's head.

Fright widened her eyes, and she visibly trembled, no doubt due to Jake's growing agitation and recklessness. He was cornered with nowhere to go. Ridge didn't believe the man would give up easily.

"Don't be a fool, Jake," the chief warned. "You won't get away with this."

"We'll see about that."

"What about Gracie and the girls?" Ridge made a desperate attempt to reason with the man. "They'd want you to surrender. At the least, they'd want you to release Elena."

Jake hesitated, but only for a moment. Whatever evil had a hold of him refused to let go.

"I'm going to walk away." He shuffled a step to the side. "And I'm taking Elena with me. If you come after us, she dies."

"I won't let you," the chief said. "I'll shoot first."

"You won't risk hitting Elena."

By then, the vehicle had arrived, its loud siren piercing the night air. The occupant—Oscar?—wouldn't be able to make it up the hill. The rugged trail barely accommodated the ATV. He would have to park at the bottom and travel the remaining distance on foot, giving Jake a five-or ten-minute head start.

"Tell Gracie I'm sorry," he said and began backing away, dragging Elena with him.

"No," she cried out, resisting.

God, don't let him take her, Ridge silently begged.

The next moment, the recognizable *thump-thump* of helicopter blades sounded, growing closer with each passing second. As the copter neared, a giant beam of light shot down from its underside. It cut a zigzag path through the brush and cacti until it found Jake and Elena. There, the helicopter hovered in the sky above them, shining its beam directly on them.

Ridge looked up and read the writing on the helicopter's side. Bisbee had sent a medical rescue team.

Jake squinted, blinded by the bright light. His hand holding the gun wavered as the gravity of the situation played across his features. And then, desperation filled his eyes.

Panic consumed Ridge. The situation had become desperate. There was no telling what his brother-in-law would do.

The chief took aim.

"Elena," Ridge hollered.

Her gaze met his across the distance separating them. He didn't know if she could see his face so he moved into the ATV's headlights.

"You can do this," he told her, hoping and praying she understood his meaning. "You can get away."

All at once, her expression changed to one of calm determination. And then, she elbowed Jake viciously in the stomach. With the swiftness of someone trained in self-defense, she twisted and threw herself to the ground where she rolled out of the way.

Jake spun and leveled his weapon at the chief.

A shot rang out, echoing in Ridge's ears.

"Elena!"

He dove toward her just as Jake dropped his gun and staggered backward, a dark circle appearing in the center of his jacket.

Complete chaos erupted. Deafening sounds and frenzied actions all occurring at once. The helicopter. Shouting. Lights. The sledgehammer inside Ridge's chest slamming into his ribs.

"Stay back!" the chief yelled.

He heard the other man as if from a distance. Reaching Elena, he dropped to his knees and scooped her into his arms. "Elena! Sweetheart. Are you all right?"

"I'm fine." Her voice shook, and her limbs trembled. "I'm fine."

"Thank God."

"What about Jake?"

Ridge looked up just as Jake, his expression crazed, hurled himself over the side of the ledge. Squeezing his eyes shut, Ridge pulled Elena closer and said a silent prayer for his sister and nieces.

Shouting preceded the arrival of Oscar, who'd parked at the bottom of the hill. The beam from the helicopter swept the ravine. Voices clamored in the background: the chief on his radio, Oscar on his, and a woman barking commands from the helicopter's loudspeaker.

Flashlights appeared, their beams racing across the ground as Oscar and the chief hurried to the ledge. Then, the beams disappeared over the edge.

"Can you spot him?" the chief hollered.

"Down there," Oscar said. "To the right."

"Is he alive?"

"Hard to tell from this distance... I think I see him moving."

The chief was back on his radio, updating someone on the situation. Overhead, the helicopter circled, aiming its light into the ravine. In the open side door, a figure stood attaching a harness. They were preparing to drop the rescue worker into the ravine.

"Can you stand?" Ridge asked Elena.

"Yes."

He helped her to her feet. She wobbled, and he tightened his hold around her waist.

Emotion filled his chest to bursting. "I… I don't… I don't know what I'd have done if anything happened to you."

"I'm okay." She clung to him.

"Are you sure?"

"Nothing a little aspirin won't remedy. He knocked me in the head."

"Let me take you to the hospital."

"That's not necessary."

"Elena, you need to be examined by a doctor."

"I'm not going anywhere until Jake's b—" She swallowed. "Until Jake is brought out." She buried her face in Ridge's jacket, a soft sob escaping. "I thought of you. When Jake had me. About what we might have had together. There were so many things I wished I'd told you."

"Shh." He enveloped her in his embrace and rested his chin on her head. "We have our whole lives ahead of us and all the time to say whatever we want."

She lifted her gaze to his. "I'm glad to hear you say that. I…care for you, Ridge. More than I believed possible."

The emotion building inside him burst free. "Good. Because I care for you, too. And if you give me half a chance, I could fall head over heels in love."

"Oh, Ridge. I feel the same—"

His lips on hers prevented her from finishing. Joy and relief and gratitude mingled and lifted their spirits higher still. Elena had survived the ordeal. She was safe in his arms. She'd admitted to returning his feelings.

Whatever challenges lay ahead, and there would be many,

they would overcome them together. Ridge believed it with every fiber of his being.

"Come on." He tugged Elena away from the ledge. "You're still shaking."

He made her sit on the ATV while they watched the rescue team workers retrieve Jake. After the medic had been lowered into the ravine, a basket was sent down. The sound of the helicopter blades combined with the chief on his radio and Oscar yelling over the side of the ledge to create a frantic cacophony.

Everything moved at high speed while at the same time seemed to take forever. At last, the basket appeared, rising from the ravine like an anchor being pulled from the ocean's depths. The basket spun in a slow circle, propelled by the wind generated from the helicopter blades.

As they watched, the basket disappeared inside the helicopter, pulled in by a crew member. The line was dropped again, and the medic retrieved. And then, the helicopter retreated from the area, executed a half-circle turn and flew off.

It was over. Their ordeal had ended.

"Elena?" Chief Dempsey materialized before her and Ridge. "How you doing?"

"I'm all right, Chief." As if to prove her point, she slid off the ATV. "What about Jake? Is he alive?"

"For the moment. What happens next is in the Lord's hands."

The chief's expression displayed only a slight change. Ridge knew the man well enough to recognize his internal struggle. He hadn't wanted to shoot Jake and had only done it to save a life. He'd be grappling with the consequences for the rest of his.

"Part of me still doesn't believe it," Elena said. "Jake was behind everything. The texts. The car tailing us. Probably whatever that thing was that flew past my back patio."

Ridge understood her disbelief. He couldn't imagine his sister and nieces' anguish when they learned what happened.

He vowed in that moment to be there for them, whatever they needed.

"Chief," he said. "Will you be the one telling Gracie?"

"Yes. I'm heading there shortly."

"I'd like to come with you."

"I was hoping you'd say that. Tomorrow, whenever you're up to it, we'll need to see you at the station to take your statement. I'm sure the Bisbee police will want to talk to you, too. They're on their way to the hospital. I'll meet them there after I've spoken to Gracie." The chief exhaled a long breath. "I think a lot of people are going to be happy to put this case to rest."

"Jake killed Pete Burnham," Elena said. She took Ridge's hand in hers, her expression filled with sorrow. "He told me everything. He's led a double life all these years."

"I'm looking forward to hearing all about that," the chief answered.

"Me, too," Ridge said.

Elena moved closer. "Would you like me to be there when you tell Gracie? To answer any questions she may have?"

Ridge squeezed her fingers, letting her know how much her sympathy and support meant to him. "Thank you, but I think the fewer people the better. Later, she may have questions for you."

"All right." Elena nodded and turned to her boss. "I'll meet you back at the station, Chief."

"You'll do no such thing." He leveled a finger at her. "You're going to the hospital."

"I'm not hurt."

"Don't play tough, Elena. Ridge told me you took a blow to the head. My guess is you have a concussion." The chief hitched his chin at Oscar, who'd been taking notes and photos with his phone. "Oscar will drive you. That's an order," he said before she could protest.

Oscar. Another person, mused Ridge, who they'd suspected and was innocent.

But was Olivia Gifford? Ridge would tell what he knew about her to the chief and the Bisbee police.

"I'll report first thing tomorrow," Elena said.

The chief shook his head. "You're on leave until admin's cleared you."

"Chief."

"Jake almost killed you. That's no small thing. You'll need counseling, even if you think you don't. You can come to the station tomorrow to give your statement and, like Ridge, talk to the Bisbee police. Not to report for duty."

"Yes, sir."

The older man reached out and clasped her shoulder. "You handled yourself well. Kept your head about you even when the situation got dicey. I'm proud of you. Your father will be, too. You have what it takes to be an excellent deputy sheriff and to go far. I mean it when I say I hope you'll stay in Iron-wood Creek."

"Thank you." Elena's words came out choked.

He nodded before leaving them to join Oscar.

Ridge let go of her hand in order to put an arm around her. "I'm proud of you, too."

They didn't have much time alone before Oscar joined them. "Chief says I'm to drive you to the hospital. Can you walk? I'm parked about a half mile down the hill. I couldn't make it any further."

"Take the ATV," Ridge said before Elena could answer. "Leave it parked at the bottom. The chief and I will walk down."

"Gotcha." Oscar gave a thumbs-up. "Ready, partner?"

"Give us a minute, will you?"

"Sure." The deputy sheriff's smile said he liked the idea of her and Ridge together.

Ridge liked it, too.

When there were just the two of them, he said, "I can meet you at the hospital later. After the chief and I have broken the news to my sister. I'll give you a ride home."

"She and your nieces are going to need you. I'll be all right. You stay with them."

"She may want to go to the hospital. To see Jake. Whatever he's done, they were married for a lot of years, and she loves him."

"I would want to be there if I were her."

"You would?"

"To make peace with myself if nothing else. Emotions are bound to be complicated at a time like this."

"Complicated is an understatement," Ridge said. "I think I'll call my mom on the way to Gracie's house. She'll probably want to stay with Gracie and the girls for a bit."

"That's a good idea. I'm sure Gracie will appreciate it." She hesitated, searching his face. "Your emotions must also be complicated. Jake is your brother-in-law."

Ridge attempted a smile. "Maybe all of us can get a group discount with the therapist."

"You joke, but that's not the worst idea." Elena closed her eyes and sighed. "I'll pray for Gracie and the girls."

"Thank you. They can use all the prayers they can get." Ridge took both of Elena's hands in his and pressed them to his chest, right over his heart. "Speaking of prayers, God answered mine when He saved you."

"Mine, too."

"He brought us together for a reason. I don't want to deny ourselves the opportunity to explore that reason."

She found his hand and squeezed his fingers. "Nor do I."

He drew her close for a kiss, not caring that the chief and Oscar stood twenty-five feet away. He'd almost lost this woman who, he believed with absolute certainty, was the one he'd been searching for his entire life.

"I'll call you as soon as I can," he said, releasing her.

Her answer was to cradle his cheek with her palm as she looked at him with the care and devotion Ridge was certain mirrored the light shining in his eyes.

The once-noisy night fell quiet around them. Tomorrow would bring a new day and the start of their life together.

Oscar came over. "You ready?"

"Yeah." Elena kissed Ridge briefly on the lips once more before climbing on the ATV.

Seeing her with the other deputy, a memory suddenly returned to Ridge, giving him cause for concern. "Hey, Oscar. Wait a sec," he said.

"What's up?"

"Why were you acting so strange that night you drove up on us behind the bank?"

"You kidding?" The deputy grinned, first at Ridge then Elena. "I was making sure she was all right. We deputies look out for each other. And the fact was, you looked pretty suspicious."

Ridge supposed he had. A moment later, he and the chief watched the two deputies disappear down the hill.

"Quite a night," the chief commented.

"Quite."

"You take care of her, Ridge. If you don't, you're going to have the entire Cochise County Sheriff's Department after you."

"You have nothing to worry about. I haven't told her yet, but I'm going to marry her one day."

The chief squeezed Ridge's shoulder, and the two of them started walking. "Glad to hear that, son. Real glad."

EPILOGUE

Six Weeks Later

Elena knelt on the ground beside Ridge. The two of them patted the earth at the base of a cluster of gold poppies they'd planted beside the well house. The flowers grew in abundance in Ironwood Creek and around the Burnham ranch. Ridge had dug up this particular cluster and transplanted them to the spot beside the well house where he'd found the gun and the strongbox.

"Before Minnie Pearl eats every wildflower on the property," he'd said earlier while digging up the flowers from behind the barn. Followed by, "Dad always liked these. Called them butterscotch blossoms."

Elena had helped Ridge construct the private memorial to his father, along with several members of Hillside Church. She recruited Mr. Harmon, who, it turned out, was a talented artist, to paint a mural on the side of the well house. He recreated the same hill where Pete Burnham had lost his life. Only rather than depicting a dark scene, the sun's rays stretched down from a vivid blue sky to bathe a soaring dove in golden light. On the ground below, three tiny, indistinguishable figures watched, their gazes raised. Elena liked to believe the figures represented Ridge, Gracie and their mom.

The image evoked feelings of love and wonder and peace.

She decided Pete Burnham would have approved, if only because it gave his family comfort. Ridge especially.

He leaned back to inspect their work. "What do you think?"

"They look great." Elena touched a delicate blossom and then placed her hand on his.

Affectionate gestures between them came naturally, as if they'd been together for years instead of weeks. Conversation, too. She was able to open up to Ridge like no one else before. They'd spent hours talking and getting to know each other. And just when she thought she might have learned everything about him, he surprised her with something new. She hoped it would be like that always for them.

Best of all, perhaps, her family adored him. After two visits, they already considered him an honorary Tomes. Elena's mom now had someone new to fuss over and feed, and her dad admired Ridge's impressive rodeo career and cattle ranching ambitions. Her siblings simply thought he was cool.

He pushed to his feet and helped her to hers.

From behind them came Gracie's voice. "Here you go."

Both Elena and Ridge turned to face his sister and mother. They'd come for this unofficial service. Gracie had brought an intricate wooden cross she'd purchased from a craftsman in Bisbee.

"Dad would like this," Ridge said and accepted the cross from her. Then, using a rubber mallet, he drove the cross into the ground, right in the center of the flowers.

Elena watched him from her place on Gracie's right. On Gracie's left stood Ridge's mom, clasping Gracie's hand in hers.

Ridge's sister needed a lot of support these days. She'd taken the news of her husband's double life and criminal history as hard as might be expected and was still struggling. Jake had survived his injuries, though it had been touch and go for days. He was currently residing in jail and awaiting his trial, having been denied bail. The prosecutor had convinced the judge that, because of his connection to the cartel, Jake was considered a flight risk.

So not only did Gracie have to contend with all that, she had to explain to her two young daughters why their daddy wasn't ever coming home again. Eventually, when they were older, she'd have to tell them what he'd done.

Elena felt nothing but sympathy and compassion for Gracie and would do whatever she could to help the woman navigate the drastic changes in her life. While Elena had initially resisted the mandatory therapy, she'd come to appreciate her sessions and seen the value. Hopefully, the support group Gracie had joined, as well as the counselor she was taking the girls to once a week, would help them, too. Ridge seemed to think so.

For now, his mother was driving from Bisbee every weekend to stay with her daughter and grandchildren. Ridge babysat them one day during the week, enabling Gracie to attend appointments with her various attorneys and financial advisor. It turned out that Jake Peterson didn't exist. That had been an identity created for him by the cartel. Which left a lot of legal issues that needed resolving, including a set of paternal grandparents Gracie hadn't realized existed and who lived in Wisconsin.

Her top priority, however, was seeing that she and her daughters had a roof over their heads and a steady source of income. Ridge had dipped into his savings and paid the first installment toward buying out her half of the ranch. More payments would follow quarterly. Additionally, they'd hired a lawyer, and their claim on the forty thousand dollars was expected to be approved in the near future. Gracie had enough to get by on until she found a job.

Gracie hadn't seen Jake since his release from the hospital. She'd yet to decide if she'd attend the trial. As that was months away, she had plenty of time to consider it. And for all anyone knew, there might not be a trial. Jake had been offered a reduced sentence in exchange for information. His lawyer was negotiating with the prosecutor.

Olivia Gifford and her family had left town. The police had questioned her extensively, learning nothing significant. Rumors abounded, however. Elena had her own suspicions.

She thought perhaps Olivia had taken a bribe from her former boss, the late mayor who was in cahoots with the cartel, in exchange for her silence regarding what she'd witnessed. That would explain her coming into money. And now that Pete Burnham's homicide had been solved, she feared retribution from the cartel and fled the area. Had she kept her mouth shut and not gotten caught up in the thrill of solving a crime like the murder mystery podcasts she liked to listen to, she might not have had to fear for her and her family's safety.

Initially, after Jake kidnapped and attempted to murder Elena, the townspeople had panicked. What if the cartel returned in full force? Clearly, they'd never really retreated. Ironwood Creek could once again become a hub for drug trafficking.

Sheriff Cochrane, whose popularity had risen in the polls since Jake's arrest and the solving of Pete Burnham's homicide, had personally visited Ironwood Creek two weeks ago and assured its citizens in a televised press conference that his crack-down-on-crime program would not only continue, but had received additional funding—a portion of which was designated to securing the area surrounding the town.

Elena had thought his press conference sounded a little like a vote-for-me-in-the-next-election speech. But, all in all, he was a good sheriff and committed to protecting her new hometown.

"That looks nice," Ridge's mom said when he'd finished with the cross, her smile melancholy. "You'll need to build a little fence to keep that donkey of yours out."

"You're probably right."

He surveyed his handiwork. The cross rose a foot above

the blooming flowers, the effect lovely. Elena was certain that Ridge and his family would visit this spot often to reflect and find comfort.

He joined Elena, his sister and his mom. They stood together, holding on to each other and contemplating the memorial.

"I'd like to say a few words about Dad," Ridge said and recounted a favorite story of Pete Burnham taking him prospecting.

His mom and then Gracie followed with their own stories. All positive. Pete had his faults, everyone there knew it, but this wasn't the time to dwell on them. They were here to celebrate the good the man had done in his life, most of which was fathering and raising two fine children. Lastly, Ridge led them in a prayer.

"Dear Lord. Thank You for Your many blessings, among them finally giving us the answers to Dad's final days and what happened. With that knowledge, we can all move on and truly forgive Dad. He was wrong to steal and wrong to believe the end justified the means. But at the core, he was a good man. A kind man. A caring man. True, he didn't always make the best decisions, and it cost him his life. We hope, in Your abundant mercy, You have forgiven him, too, and welcomed him into Your heavenly kingdom. We ask that You stay by our sides as we move ahead in our lives after Jake's betrayal. We rely on Your guidance and Your love. Today and every day. Amen."

A chorus of amens followed.

It was, Elena thought, a fine and fitting memorial.

"We should get going." Ridge's mom glanced at her watch. "When do you have to be there?"

"Four o'clock," Elena said. She was receiving a commendation today in a ceremony at Ironwood Creek town hall. She felt she'd just been doing her job, but the chief insisted she'd gone above and beyond and deserved recognition. "And I need to go home and change first."

They all four started down the rise. At the house, Elena hugged Gracie and Ridge's mom, confirming they would see one another in a couple hours.

"How's the new deputy doing?" Ridge asked at her car.

"He's all right." She laughed. "The best part is I don't have to patrol the pecan orchard anymore."

"Does that mean you're going to apply for sergeant deputy when Oscar retires in a couple of years?"

The senior deputy had been given the position after Jake's arrest.

"Absolutely." Elena sent Ridge a questioning look. "You won't have a problem with that, will you?"

"Not at all. I rather like the idea of being married to a career law enforcement officer."

"Married!"

"Not for a while." He lowered his lips to her for a warm kiss. "Just letting you know that's on the table for someday."

"I'm glad. I love you, Ridge."

"I love you, too."

Any doubts Elena once had about balancing a career and a husband and children had vanished, chased away by the strength of Ridge's feelings for her. Turned out, she'd just needed to meet the right man.

Thanks to God's many blessings, she had. The past was behind them, and a long life filled with happiness and promise awaited. She need only gaze into Ridge's handsome face to know he was on this journey with her every step of the way.

* * * * *

HARLEQUIN
Reader Service

Enjoyed your book?

Try the perfect subscription for Romance readers and get more great books like this delivered right to your door.

See why over 10+ million readers have tried Harlequin Reader Service.

Start with a Free Welcome Collection with free books and a gift—valued over $20.

Choose any series in print or ebook. See website for details and order today:

TryReaderService.com/subscriptions